Lara found herself suddenly stammering at his touch, "is because you're a man."

"I'm a man. Well, that's certainly news," Miles murmured teasingly, and continued to stroke Lara's hair.

"What I . . . what I mean is well, well—" Lara actually felt a shiver when Miles's fingers brushed against the nape of her neck "—uh, that is, a man has the advantage because he is traditionally taller and stronger."

"Is that so?" Miles's breath fanned her moist cheek.

Lara suppressed a quiver as she savored the unexpectedly tantalizing closeness. "So maybe the race wasn't exactly fair and square after all." Her voice came out sounding slightly higher.

"Things seldom are fair." Miles's mouth hovered scant inches above her own.

For one dizzying instant, Lara thought he was about to kiss her. "Miles, I—"

"You *what* Lara?" he whispered hoarsely, his lips continuing their slow, inevitable descent.

He *was* going to kiss her, Lara realized with delicious anticipation. Any moment now, that hard, firm mouth would capture her own and she would finally know after all these years what it would be like to be kissed by Miles Crane. . . .

Dear Reader,

Happy Spring! It's May, the flowers are blooming and love is in the air. It's the month for romance—both discovery and renewal—the month for mothers and the time of new birth. It's a wonderful time of year!

And in this special month, we have some treats in store for you. Silhouette Romance's DIAMOND JUBILEE is in full swing, and *Second Time Lucky* by Victoria Glenn is bound to help you get into the springtime spirit. Lovely heroine Lara discovers that sometimes love comes from unexpected sources when she meets up with handsome, enigmatic Miles. Don't miss this tender tale! Then, in June, *Cimarron Knight*, the first book in Pepper Adams's exciting new trilogy—*CIMARRON STORIES*—will be available. Set on the plains of Oklahoma, these three books are a true delight.

The DIAMOND JUBILEE—Silhouette Romance's tenth anniversary celebration—is our way of saying thanks to you, our readers. To symbolize the timelessness of love, as well as the modern gift of the tenth anniversary, we're presenting readers with a DIAMOND JUBILEE Silhouette Romance title each month, penned by one of your favorite Silhouette Romance authors. In the coming months writers such as Marie Ferrarella, Lucy Gordon, Dixie Browning, Phyllis Halldorson—to name just a few—are writing DIAMOND JUBILEE titles especially for you.

And that's not all! Laurie Paige has a heartwarming duo coming up—*Homeward Bound*. The first book, *A Season for Homecoming*, is coming your way in June. Peggy Webb also has *Venus de Molly*, a sequel to *Harvey's Missing*, due out in July. And much-loved Diana Palmer has some special treats in store during the months ahead....

I hope you'll enjoy this book and all of the stories to come. Come home to romance—Silhouette Romance—for always!

Sincerely,
Tara Hughes Gavin
Senior Editor

VICTORIA GLENN

Second Time Lucky

Silhouette ❦ *Romance*

Published by Silhouette Books New York

America's Publisher of Contemporary Romance

SILHOUETTE BOOKS
300 E. 42nd St., New York, N.Y. 10017

Copyright © 1990 by Victoria Dann

ISBN: 0-373-08718-7

First Silhouette Books printing May 1990

VICTORIA GLENN,

an award-winning writer herself, comes from a family of writers. She makes her home in the Connecticut countryside, but divides her time between the East and West Coasts. She considers it essential to the creative process to visit Disneyland at least twice a year.

A Note From The Author:

Dear Reader:

This special Diamond Jubilee Celebration means a great deal to me, personally. I have been reading Silhouette Romances long before I ever began writing them. And I can even remember a time in the not-so-distant past when it was nearly impossible to find a modern romance novel in most bookstores. Those of us searching for a satisfactory love story had to be contented with a few pages here or there within the confines of other genres. Needless to say, the experience was far from satisfactory. Happily, however, the modern love story has at last come into its own. No longer is romance merely a subplot, but a glorious, wonderful adventure, complete in itself. And in this way, art truly *does* imitate life. For is there any adventure more thrilling, suspenseful or so supremely enjoyable as love? And what makes romance so very wonderfully exciting is the knowledge that it can happen to anyone of us . . . at any time. Today, or even tomorrow, it could happen to you.

Sincerely,
Victoria Glenn

Chapter One

The man waiting in the baggage claim area hadn't changed much in six years. It wasn't just the blond hair still cropped unfashionably short, or those same cynical lines around his hard gray eyes. There also remained that odd air of formality about Miles Crane, an almost mournful reserve that went far beyond the somber suits he always wore. It was hard to believe he was Jason's brother.

Jason. Even now, Lara's heart lurched at the very thought of him. Handsome, reckless Jason Crane, who had taught her all about pain and betrayal. Laughing, vital Jason Crane. The only man she had ever loved.

Determinedly she forced those thoughts from her mind. Jason no longer existed. The years had wiped him from her life with a gentle hand. And this man standing in the bright lobby of Kennedy Airport was as different from his younger brother as night was from day.

"Miles." She pushed away from the other arriving passengers and greeted him with an enthusiastic hug.

His body stiffened slightly. "Welcome home, Lara," he murmured in surprise, but didn't pull away from the unexpected embrace.

Belatedly Lara realized she had made a mistake. In all the time she had known him, Lara had never openly displayed any affection for Miles. Her gesture had been an unconscious one. After all, she had spent the past six years in southern California where warm hugs and casual kisses were commonplace. Awkwardly Lara drew back from the impromptu embrace. How odd, the thought occurred to her. Miles' tense body had felt so unexpectedly warm against hers. And he seemed taller than she remembered.

"Lara," he said in a deep, quiet voice. "How was your flight?"

"Oh, fine." She cleared her throat quickly. "Thanks for picking me up."

Miles stared at her strangely for a long moment. "No thanks are necessary. You're the one who's really doing the favor, Lara." He paused. "I can't tell you how much I appreciate this."

"How *is* your aunt?"

Miles compressed his lips. "Not good, I'm afraid. It means a lot to her that you've come."

"Of course I'd come. I love Lizbeth." Lara couldn't help the slight indignation in her tone, which was more a reaction to Miles's hesitant words. She'd been able to read question in his eyes. He had clearly believed she might not have come back at all, despite her tender feelings for the elderly woman who was her godmother. After all, Lara had been gone for six years. In all that time she had never once considered the possibility of returning to Pine Harbor. The memories of that fateful day with Jason were still too painful. Why should she be foolish enough to dredge up the past? That part of her life was gone forever. The one part of the sad equation Lara hadn't reckoned with had been Jason's Aunt Lizbeth. "Of course I'd come," Lara repeated softly, more to herself than to Miles.

He didn't say anything for a moment. Then as if to clear some disturbing emotion from his mind, he nodded in the direction of the luggage carousel. "Let's get your suitcases."

Lara shrugged and gestured down at the compact garment bag she had carried off the plane. It had been flung carelessly to the floor when she'd given him the hug. "That's it, Miles. I don't have any suitcases."

He twisted his lips. "Well now. That's interesting."

"What do you mean?"

"As I recall—" he leaned over and picked up the canvas bag effortlessly "—you never traveled anywhere without at least three suitcases."

She looked up at him. "I think you exaggerate."

Miles shook his head. "The Lara MacEuan I used to know had an outfit for every hour of the day."

"Well, I'm not exactly the person I used to be," Lara replied quietly.

"I can see that," came the soft reply. His enigmatic silver eyes flickered over her body. If Lara had been able to read his mind she might have been more than just a bit surprised. Miles was thinking that Lara MacEuan was even lovelier than he remembered. Now, she was more than the pretty teenager who had turned the heads of everyone in town. In the past six years, she had become a beautiful young woman. There were new curves beneath the snug denim jeans and pink cotton sweater. The wild mane of brown hair, which had once hung past her waist, now barely brushed her shoulder in shiny waves. A distinct and exceedingly attractive improvement, Miles decided. And her huge hazel eyes still had the power to astonish him, but now there was a sadness in their depths. Miles twisted his mouth in annoyance. He knew just who had put that sadness there. Was there ever a time Jason *hadn't* been responsible for somebody's unhappiness? All the time in the world couldn't change that, he thought bitterly. And what had been his own role in all of this? He was Jason's big brother. From the time he was seven years old, it seemed he had always been tidying up after Jason. And when it came to Lara—Miles stopped himself abruptly. He'd better not think about Lara right now. The thoughts he'd been having about her all these years had very nearly gotten him into serious trouble.

"I said, come back here this minute!" a shrill voice suddenly pierced the air. Heads turned. "Come back here before I give you the spanking of your life!" the voice warned. "Joey, do you hear me?"

As if on cue, something small and bubbling with energy hurled itself through the crowd. The rambunctious little Joey who was about three years old, eluded his grown-up pursuer with almost demonic speed and skill, the trademarks of any average mischievous child.

In less than an instant, little Joey had collided with the canvas carryall, stumbled over Miles Crane's expensive black leather oxfords and tumbled into a bewildered heap at Lara's feet. Although completely unharmed, the child began to wail like a banshee.

Immediately Lara knelt down on the hard floor and began to comfort the crying youngster. "Are you all right, sweetheart?" she murmured in her most gentle consoling tone. There was nothing more troubling to Lara than the sight of a weeping child.

"'I fell!" Joey whined plaintively in between noisy sobs. "I fell!"

"Yes, I know." Lara nodded soothingly and touched the toddler's shoulder. "Why don't we find your mommy?"

Miles had been watching the brief exchange with an odd expression on his gaunt face, his arms crossed in front of his chest. "I think Mommy has arrived," he suddenly remarked with faint amusement.

Joey's mother was a tiny woman in a loose-fitting Hawaiian print shift, with a short helmet of lacquered red hair and a sunburn to match. And the clarion voice that had blasted its way across the terminal was ten times more ear-shattering at close range. "Didn't I tell you not to run?" came the shrill warning. There was the sound of a sharp slap and little Joey began crying at the top of his lungs again. Then the woman gripped her child's hand angrily and narrowed her eyes at Lara. "And he's not supposed to talk to strangers!" Without another word, with Joey in tow, the woman in the muumuu stalked away.

"Wonderful mother," Miles murmured wryly.

"What an unpleasant person!" Lara shook her head in disbelief. "That poor little boy!"

"I feel sorry for *both* of them," Miles remarked with a shake of his head.

"The nerve of that lady." Lara stared off into the distance at the two retreating figures. "Here I was, trying to help a little boy who might have injured himself.... She spoke to me as if I were some kind of criminal!"

"Well, it's obvious that one thing about you hasn't changed, Lara MacEuan," her companion observed quietly.

"What do you mean?"

"Apparently you still expect the best from people."

"That's not quite true," Lara protested.

"You know you do." Miles gave a weary smile. "And you're inevitably disappointed." The moment the words were out of his mouth, Miles regretted having said them. But it was too late to take the words back.

"I guess you're right." A shadow passed across Lara's face for just a moment. There was an uncomfortable silence.

Cursing himself inwardly for his blunder, Miles reached for the carryall and hoisted it on his shoulder once more. He hadn't meant to hurt Lara's feelings, but then he was always an insensitive idiot when it came to women and their feelings. Lara must have instantly assumed he had been referring to Jason and her blind belief in him, even after his agonizing betrayal. The expression on Lara's face told Miles how painful that betrayal still was after six long years.

He cleared his throat. "We'd better get going if we want to beat the rush hour traffic."

"Of course," Lara agreed hastily. Well, there it was. The shadow of Jason Crane. Any illusions she'd had about the ghosts of her past not coming back to haunt her during this brief visit were completely dissolved now. The pity she had seen in Miles's eyes six years ago was the same pity he had tried so vainly to conceal just now. The last thing Lara wanted—she pressed her lips together firmly—was pity from anyone. Lara quickened her pace to keep up with Miles.

They did not exchange a single word as the two of them emerged from the automatic sliding doors of the sleek terminal building and began to make their way cautiously between streams of traffic toward the parking area. It was a muggy July afternoon. Even though Lara was used to heat after years of living in Los Angeles, the oppressive humidity in New York was a different matter altogether. The moisture hung heavy in the air. If this weather was any indication, she gave an inward sigh, it was going to be a distinctly uncomfortable visit.

"It's right over here." Miles's voice suddenly intruded on her thoughts. He gestured in the direction of a familiar tan Mercedes. It was the same car he had driven six years ago.

Lara stood quietly as Miles opened the passenger door. "Oh," she murmured suddenly. There was genuine amazement in her tone. "You kept it."

"Kept what? You mean the car?"

"No, not the car."

Puzzled, Miles followed her glance toward the small white tassel dangling from the rearview mirror. It was from the mortarboard that went with Lara's high school graduation cap and gown. Strange, he'd almost forgotten it was there. It had become so much a part of the car. "Oh that," he murmured vaguely. "You hung it up there yourself, remember?" He shut the door behind her and stowed the carryall in the trunk.

As he slid his lanky frame into the driver's seat, Lara's new rush of memories began. She recalled the night after graduation when she'd hung the tassel up in this very same car, in a gesture of hurt defiance against Jason. He had been supposed to take her to the senior class party and had never shown up. At the eleventh hour Miles had appeared, somewhat angry and apologetic, to act as her last-minute escort. "I don't want to go," she had declared tremulously.

Miles, standing there in his usual somber suit, had shaken his head firmly. "It's your graduation dance. It's important to you. And you're going." Without another word, he had handed her a hastily purchased corsage and guided her down the steps to his waiting car.

Recalling it now, Lara thought of what a strange night that had been. Miles had been so much older than everyone else at the dance, except for one or two fathers who had escorted their dateless daughters. He'd danced every dance with her that night, even the fast ones, and it had been an odd sight, indeed. Miles Crane dancing. Even during such an activity he still managed to look somber, particularly during the slow music. He'd held her so stiffly, almost awkwardly, as if dancing was not an exercise he was very much at ease with.

"You *do* remember, don't you?" Miles' voice brought Lara back to the present.

She nodded. "Yes, I remember." There was a long pause. What was there to say to a person you had scarcely spoken to in six years? Up until several days ago, she hadn't given Miles Crane a second thought. Out of the blue, he had phoned her in Los Angeles, an almost poignant urgency in his tone. His great-aunt

Lizbeth was seriously ill and had been asking for her.
Yes, of course, he realized that it was a major incon-
venience to ask Lara to drop everything and fly back
to Pine Harbor. Tactfully Miles hadn't mentioned it
would also be extremely painful. She had sworn never
to return to her hometown on the shores of southern
Connecticut. Not after all that had happened. But now
that bitterness must be set aside for the sake of Lizbeth Crane, the ailing woman who had loved Lara as
if she was her own granddaughter. It had been Lizbeth who had suffered the most when Jason left Lara
at the altar six years ago. For Lizbeth, who had never
married, the wedding of her favorite nephew to Lara
MacEuan had been planned ever since the two of them
were toddlers. Who could ever have foreseen the mis-
ery that eventually unfolded? And who even knew
where Jason was now?

"No—" Miles practically read her thoughts "—I
haven't heard from him in six months. Nobody has."

"How did you—" Lara began, then stopped herself. What was the use of trying to hide her feelings?
"It's not that I care anymore." She felt it was necessary to explain.

"I'm sure you don't," he interjected grimly.

"I merely was curious, that's all," Lara insisted.

"Of course," came the crisp retort.

She floundered for a moment, staring blindly out
the window as the scenery raced past them on the
thruway. "He could be dead, for all I know."

Miles shot her a sharp glance. "I doubt that he's dead, Lara. People like Jason always land on their feet." Unconsciously his hard fingers gripped the steering wheel even tighter. He thought of the last postcard he'd received from his wayward younger brother. Dashed off in his usual careless hand from another exotic port, this time somewhere in Malaysia. *Merry Christmas and a happy New Year!* it had declared cheerfully. Miles cleared his throat now. "So, tell mc about yourself, Lara. I understand you've been very successful with your writing."

He hadn't exactly changed the subject with great deftness, she thought with wry amusement, but then Miles had never been known for his subtlety. "My writing? Oh, I do all right." Lara shrugged.

He gave her a sideways glance. "Oh, you've been doing more than just 'all right,' Lara MacEuan. I see your name on the credits of the *Hap Harrigan* series every week." Miles paused. "It's a funny show. But then, you were always very talented."

She stared back at him in surprise. "I never knew you felt that way."

He quirked an eyebrow. "What did you believe I thought, Lara? That you were some kind of airhead with nothing behind that pretty face of yours?"

"Frankly, yes." Maybe just the "airhead" part, Lara amended silently. It had never occurred to her that Miles Crane might have thought her pretty. So why was his backhanded compliment causing the strangest sensation in the pit of her stomach?

"I never thought that for a moment," Miles was saying. "I always knew you were capable of great things, Lara. Just look at all you've accomplished out there in Los Angeles."

It was downright embarrassing to sit in the car as it headed toward New England and listen to Miles make such flattering remarks about her. In fact it was almost weird. She had known him practically since the day she was born, yet this was the first time the man had spoken to Lara as if she was an adult instead of some hopeless adolescent. If he had ever thought her capable of "great things," he'd never before given the slightest clue as to his true feelings.

Even as a teenager, he'd seemed so dour and restrained. She remembered Miles at eighteen, going off to the same Ivy League college that generations of Cranes had attended before him. He had been so serious and determined. He was going to be a lawyer; there had never been a trace of doubt in his mind. Through the eyes of a seven-year-old girl, Miles had resembled the bookworms she'd always seen in cartoons, with a bowtie and horn-rimmed glasses. Those glasses were gone now, Lara couldn't help but notice. He had obviously gotten contact lenses. No longer were those enigmatic, silver eyes concealed. What interesting eyes Miles Crane had. Whoa! Just wait a minute. Since when had she given two seconds' thought to Miles Crane and his eyes?

"What's wrong with me?" Miles interrupted her reverie.

"Excuse me?"

"You've been staring in my direction for the past three minutes," he remarked quietly. "I was just wondering if it was something particularly drastic. Do I have a spider on my head, Lara?"

It never occurred to him, Lara thought, that she might be staring at *him*, just for the sake of it. Frankly it had never occurred to Lara, either, until this very moment. For some bizarre reason, she suddenly noticed he had become an attractive man. Or, even a more bewildering possibility, Miles Crane had always been attractive and she had simply never realized this fact before. Perhaps for the first time in her life, she wasn't comparing him to his brother. Strange. Out of the shadow of Jason, Miles didn't seem quite as drab. No. Lara's glance shifted to the angular jaw, then downward to the hard, tanned hands where they gripped the leather steering wheel. Miles had an undeniable masculinity. A quiet strength.

"All right, I give up," her companion admitted, totally mystified. "Did you notice five hundred gray hairs, a bald spot or *what*, Lara?"

"Of course not!" she retorted. "Can't a person just *look* at another person for absolutely no reason at all? Honestly, what's the big deal? I haven't seen you in six years, for goodness' sake!"

Miles reacted to this unusually prolonged outburst with an arch of one eyebrow. "Is that what you were doing? Just . . . staring?'

"Sure." She shrugged. "Is there something wrong with that?"

"No, not at all." He wrinkled his forehead pensively, an odd note in his voice. "Stare all you want." Miles had to force himself to concentrate on the traffic ahead. He had never been the object of such deliberate scrutiny, at least not from Lara. It was difficult to describe the sensations such female scrutiny aroused. And from a most unexpected source; Lara MacEuan, of all people! His fingers actually tensed at the wheel. In the past two weeks, the world had gone topsy-turvy. His great-aunt Lizbeth had had yet another relapse, a freak water-main rupture in the center of town had very nearly destroyed his law offices, and now Lara had come back to Pine Harbor. And for the very first time in all her twenty-four years, she was looking at Miles the way a woman was supposed to look at a man. It was more than just a little disconcerting. It was downright nerve shattering.

Chapter Two

The Crane family had inhabited the same Victorian house for over a century. Overlooking the silver-blue water of the Long Island Sound, it had been built by one of the Crane ancestors who was, like so many other residents of Pine Harbor back then, a retired sea captain. It was an exquisite example of the architecture of the period, with special touches added by Captain Ezra Crane himself. Painted a pristine white, the home rose to three stories, with a charming "widow's walk" running along the flattened roof. And inside, it was filled with treasures collected from the old captain's many voyages. Everything from a table crafted from a single giant tree trunk, to a rare crystal chandelier rumored to have hung in a maharajah's palace, and a giant mahogany sea chest Ezra

Crane once swore had belonged to the infamous Morgan the Pirate. As a child, Lara recalled what a wonderfully magical place the mansion had been in which to play.

But now as she entered the magnificent master bedroom and stared down at the fragile figure of Lizbeth Crane, who lay propped up against the pillows of the ebony four-poster bed, the old house was no longer wonderful or magical. All Lara could think of was how the past six years had taken their toll on this once spirited, vital woman. It wasn't just the delicate features, even more lined and drawn than Lara had remembered. It was the way Lizbeth Crane seemed to stare out of the wide picture window with unseeing blue eyes.

Miles, who had preceded Lara into the room, now sat down on the edge of the bed and gently clasped the woman's thin hand. "Aunt, look who's here!"

"Do we have company?"

"Yes, Aunt," he answered with tenderness that Lara had never thought him capable of. "We have very special company."

Lizbeth Crane seemed suddenly disturbed. "Oh, please! Send them away, Miles! I can't have company. I look a fright today! Send them away. Be a good boy like you always are."

"But just look who it is, Aunt," he insisted. "Just look!" Miles gestured for Lara to move closer. "It's Lara!"

Slowly, as her great-nephew's words began to register in her mind, the elderly woman's head turned. "Lara?" she repeated disbelievingly. "Little Lara MacEuan?"

Lara forced a smile and edged closer toward the bed. "Yes, Aunt Lizbeth, it's me."

"Oh." Tears began to film in Lizbeth Crane's eyes. "Oh, Lara. You've come back to us at last!" She reached out with a blue-veined hand to clasp her goddaughter's fingers.

Lara wasn't quite sure how to answer. Her feelings were in such a mad jumble. She only knew what mattered was that this dear, sweet person could become well again. Even if she had to lie about coming home. "Yes," Lara murmured, "I've come back."

"Isn't this wonderful news, Miles?" Lizbeth exclaimed softly, her pale face suddenly transformed with delight. "Our Lara is back home where she belongs! Aren't you pleased, dear?"

"Yes, Aunt." Miles nodded in assent. "It's wonderful news and—" he glanced over at Lara with a grateful expression in his eyes "—I'm very pleased, indeed."

"The important thing is that you're going to get well," Lara interjected hastily. She was flooded with regret and even a degree of guilt. Despite the unfortunate episode with Jason, how on earth had she ever managed to stay away for so long? Particularly when someone cared as deeply for her as Lizbeth Crane did. The change in the elderly woman's demeanor when she realized her beloved goddaughter had actually returned spoke volumes. Lara felt ashamed of her prolonged absence.

"The important thing is that you've come home, Lara," Lizbeth countered with a faint smile. Already the woman seemed to have recovered some of her old strength.

"I'm afraid this has been a bit much for you, Aunt," Miles murmured gently. "Lara and I are going to let you get some rest."

"Don't be a fuddy-duddy, Miles!" Lizbeth protested.

He shrugged. "If somebody has to be a fuddy-duddy, it might as well be me."

The older woman seemed to consider this logic for a moment, then gave a resigned sigh. "All right, then." She smiled dazzlingly at Lara. "Don't let him bully you, dear."

"Absolutely not." She nodded solemnly, and kissed Lizbeth on her withered cheek.

"I have no intention of bullying Lara," Miles declared assertively.

"Hmm," his great aunt murmured. "I doubt that."

"She's had a long, tiring plane trip, Aunt. And all I intend to do is make sure she gets a chance to rest and unpack before dinner." He paused. "If that is considered being a bully, then I plead guilty as charged."

Even in that brief exchange, Lara was engulfed by the remembered warmth of the Crane family. How she had missed being part of that special circle, and its all-encompassing aura. The past six years had brought her some degree of success, but the everyday give-and-take of normal family life had been sorely absent. It was the price she'd paid when she fled Pine Harbor and the memory of Jason's betrayal. Looking back on it now, she realized she had left behind more than just unhappy memories. There was an entire childhood filled with joy and love in the Crane household. For the fact was that Lara had actually spent more time in the rambling Crane mansion than in her own house. Michael and Arlene Crane, Jason and Miles's parents, had been affectionate and attentive to young Lara. It was hard to believe that almost twenty years had passed since Michael and Arlene had been killed in an automobile accident while on vacation in Europe.

"After dinner we'll come up and see you, Aunt," Miles was saying, "but right now, I think you should get some rest." He gestured at the private duty nurse who had spent the past few minutes sitting discreetly on the far side of the large room. The rather plump, kindly woman gave a nod and put down the magazine she had been reading.

"Time for your medication, Miss Crane," the nurse announced cheerfully.

"I'd rather have a glass of sherry," Lizbeth grumbled disparagingly.

"Wouldn't we all," the nurse agreed good-naturedly, then glanced at Miles and Lara. "I can't get over the change in her!" she marveled. "Look at the color in her cheeks. This is absolutely remarkable."

"Not when you consider the cause," Miles said with a meaningful look at Lara. "It makes perfect sense to me." And then, leaving the nurse to administer to her patient, he and Lara left the room.

Once out in the hallway, he shook his head with wonderment. "I couldn't ask for anything better than this, Lara. You're just what the doctor ordered. The improvement in her is miraculous, more than I could have hoped for."

"How long has she been like ... this?" Lara looked over her shoulder through the door, which had been left ajar.

"You mean, the way her mind wanders?" Miles sighed. "On and off for about the last year. She suffered another mild stroke last Christmas but—" he paused significantly "—the specialists all seem to think she should have improved before now. It's their opinion that the obstacle on her road to recovery is more psychological than anything else."

"Psychological?"

"I didn't agree with them until now."

"What do you mean?"

Miles's silver stare met hers. "You know exactly what I mean, Lara. Just look at the difference a few minutes with you has made in her mental attitude. She's already sharper, more alert." He compressed his lips in a hard line. "I should have sent for you sooner."

"Yes, you should have."

He gazed down at the polished oak floor with distinct uneasiness. "I wasn't sure you'd come."

Lara rolled her eyes in exasperation. "Miles, are we going to go through *that* again?"

In a gesture somewhat out of character for the rather reserved man standing next to her, he suddenly reached out and touched Lara on the shoulder. "I didn't know *then*, Lara. I know now."

"Good." Somehow she was able to find her voice. How strange to feel Miles's warmth through the thin material of her pink cotton sweater. Warmth was not exactly the first word that came to mind when one thought of Miles Crane. Odd, but Lara's previous assessment of her longtime acquaintance was beginning to change significantly. Was it remotely possible that the man she and Jason had nicknamed Serious Mister Robot might be human after all?

Just as this disturbing new thought began to percolate through Lara's mind, Miles dropped his hand abruptly. "I've got some business to take care of back in the office." He hesitated. "We can have dinner together, if you'd like."

"Sure, that's fine," she answered vaguely.

Miles fumbled almost awkwardly for his automobile keys. "I'm glad you're back, Lara." Without another word, he turned on his heel and strode toward the main staircase.

A new flood of memories assaulted Lara's senses as she unpacked her carryall in the guest bedroom. Actually there were several guest bedrooms in the Crane house, and it was a coincidence that Lara had been allotted this particular one. For this was a room in which Lara had spent a great deal of her childhood. Nor was it a coincidence that the pink rosebud-patterned wallpaper and matching coverlet on the canopied bed had been especially chosen for a little girl. This room had been decorated with Lara Mac-Euan in mind. Even now when she opened the ward-robe door, she realized with a pang of recognition that some of her old dresses still hung there in a tidy row. Bless her godmother, Lizbeth. It was as if the woman could not bear to part with those cherished memories of happier days. Covered in plastic was the white dress from Lara's sweet sixteen party, the wool pullover from her high school cheerleader outfit, and what was this? Lara reached out and pulled the plastic from a short pink sundress. Strange, she couldn't remember owning such an outfit. Frowning, she covered the dress again. Well, it wasn't as if this closet and room were her own special property. She was forgetting that six years had passed. Surely there had been other guests in this room. But until six years ago—Lara gave a weary sigh and sat down on the edge of the bed. More memories began to flow as if a floodgate had been opened.

The two most powerful families in the seaside town of Pine Harbor were the Cranes and the MacEuans. It seemed this had always been so, because no one in the village could remember otherwise. All the money, the prestige and social activity, seemed to reside within these two old families. Lara's great-grandfather, Torquil MacEuan, had made his fortune importing sugar and rum. Yes, it had been quite a fortune. Lara gave another sigh and kicked off her scuffed sneakers. She had grown up surrounded by wealth and privilege, and had realized early on that such trappings could be quite meaningless. Her own parents had very little time for Lara. It seemed that Denise and Willy MacEuan's only interest was their forty-two-foot racing yacht *Trade Winds*. Even in Lara's earliest memories of her parents, they were sunburned and smiling, kissing her goodbye as they left on another adventure. Two children who had never grown up, was what she had once overheard Lizbeth Crane grumble. But actually, the woman had always been rather delighted that her goddaughter would be left in her care so frequently. Not only did Lara represent the child she could never have, but Lara was also a MacEuan. This made her even more special to Lizbeth Crane's heart. Years ago she had loved one of Torquil MacEuan's sons, but the young man had died tragically before the wedding. This was a blow from which Lizbeth had never recovered.

Lara shook her head. Every time she thought of the misfortune her godmother had suffered, it made her own self-pity seem rather shameful. After all, it was far worse to lose a lover tragically than to simply have him desert you on your wedding day. Like Jason.

She was five years old when Lara realized she was in love with Jason Crane. He was eight-and-a-half years old and already a blond, blue-eyed dynamo. Lara's parents had continued to leave her at the Crane household more and more in those days, and Jason was delighted to recruit a new partner in his mischievous antics. Together the two of them scuffed the elegant banisters and shattered priceless antique vases as they battled pirates and fended off killer sharks. Oh, the wild imaginations of their combined young minds. But by the time she was fifteen, and Jason had gone off to college, all Lara could think about was the magical day that Jason would come home on holiday, take one look at his childhood playmate and suddenly realize that she was all grown up. He would give a startled gasp of amazement and then— Abruptly, Lara shut the floodgate of memories. What was the point of remembering those things, anyhow? So what if that particular girlhood fantasy had come true? What difference did it make that when Lara was sixteen Jason *had* come home for Christmas break and saw what to his eyes was a new and alluring Lara MacEuan? What difference did it make that he had kissed her for the first time that Christmas Eve under the mistletoe in the Crane living room—and everything between two childhood pals had from that moment changed forever? So what if the two years that followed the wonderful Christmas discovery had been the happiest Lara would ever know? Two years of knowing that the boy she loved loved her in return, and that the future was assured. Her destiny was clear. After high school graduation, Lara MacEuan would become Mrs. Jason Crane.

No, this had to stop. Lara pressed her lips in a hard line. She couldn't go on this way, thinking about the past. It was over. High time she started thinking about the future. That is, if Lara could only survive the present. The next two weeks in Pine Harbor would be very difficult and painful.

Miles joined Lara for dinner an hour later. Surprisingly it was a pleasant low-key meal served in the informal dining nook that overlooked the garden. More nostalgia, Lara thought resignedly, remembering all the Sunday morning breakfasts she had shared in this very room with Jason and Lizbeth. How the two youngsters had tried the gentle spinster's patience with their unruly pancake fights and assorted other childish behavior. For the most part, Miles had been absent from the scene. By then he was at university, and his appearances were restricted to holidays and special family occasions. In any case, Miles had never seemed to have much patience for his younger brother and the far younger Lara. In fact he took great pains to ignore them entirely. Lara had the impression the elder Crane considered them immature and hopelessly ill-behaved.

Sitting here now with Miles, as the two of them had their dessert and coffee, Lara realized this was the first time in her life she had shared a meal alone with him.

"What are you thinking about, Lara?" he asked quietly.

"Nothing," she replied evasively. Usually, Lara didn't have a problem staring people in the eye or answering them in a direct manner. But Miles was different, and she didn't know why. It was baffling.

"I had the distinct impression that you were thinking about something," Miles observed, and set down his coffee mug with deliberate precision.

"Nothing important," she tossed back. "If you must know, I was thinking that this is the first time I've sat at this table with you, without Jason and Aunt Lizbeth."

Miles stared at her steadily. "Is that so? Well, I suppose if a person lives long enough, he or she can experience everything."

The casual delivery of this remark surprised Lara. She'd never considered Miles possessed even the slightest sense of humor. "I guess," she replied lamely. Wonderful, Lara thought to herself. Here she was, a semi-successful comedy writer, and the art of simple witty dinner conversation now eluded her completely. Back in Los Angeles, Lara would have enjoyed the thrust and parry of clever repartee, but here with Miles Crane, the sharp funny retorts simply refused to bounce off her tongue. Maybe she was just tired or something. That had to be the reason. Jet lag, surely that was it.

"I want to make sure I understand this, Lara," Miles was saying. "You'll be able to spend an entire two weeks with us?"

"Yes."

"Don't think I'm not grateful, but the fact is I'm also amazed that you were able to drop everything at such short notice."

Lara shrugged. "It's no big deal, Miles." Actually, it *was* a big deal. Even though the *Hap Harrigan* series was in summer hiatus at the moment, Lara had been about to begin work on a comedy special starring some of her favorite television stars. It would have been a marvelous opportunity, a chance to break out of the weekly series grind and into a fresh new area. That's what a writer was supposed to do, and it always served to further his or her budding career. Versatil-ity. But then she had received the unexpected telephone call from Miles and everything changed. The producers of the comedy special were sympathetic, but business was business. Time was money, and all the other old clichés. They couldn't afford any delay in production whatsoever. Not a week. Not a weekend. Not even a day. So Lara did what she had to do. She bowed out of the plum assignment and took the next plane back to the East Coast. She now had the entire month of July. *The Hap Harrigan Show* wouldn't be starting up production again until August.

"Why do I get the impression that you're not telling me everything, Lara?" Miles prodded gently.

At that moment, all the frustration and bitterness that had been welling up inside Lara for the past six years suddenly gave way. "Excuse me, but I didn't realize that I was under any obligation to tell you *any-thing*, let alone everything, Miles Crane!"

He raised a startled eyebrow. "I guess that answers my question."

Oh, the man was still so infernally aggravating! He always managed to size up a situation. In his own quiet calm way, Miles Crane was able to see everything. *Mr. Know-it-All*, Jason had called him. Just another from a long list of nicknames with which he had disparaged his solemn-eyed sibling. But as much as Lara hated to admit Jason had been right about anything, the fact remained that Miles always *had* acted like an aloof, superior know-it-all. But that was no excuse for her rudeness or her impatience. She wasn't in Pine Harbor for any other reason but to see Lizbeth Crane, and there was no point in alienating Miles. She sighed. "I'm sorry I snapped at you just now. It's been a long day."

His mouth twisted. "I'm used to you snapping at me, Lara. I kind of missed it after all these years."

She was taken aback. It never occurred to Lara that Miles would miss anything about her, particularly her sharp tongue. "I never realized it until now," she confessed somewhat shamefacedly, "but I suppose I was rather bratty and obnoxious to you in the old days."

He shrugged. "Actually, I found you rather lively and high-spirited."

"The word is obnoxious, Miles. I was obnoxious, admit it."

"You were amusing, Lara."

She rolled her eyes as image after image of her unruly behavior passed through her consciousness. The time she and Jason glued all of Miles's notebooks to the top of his desk. The time they placed a pail of water over the top of Miles's bedroom door, and the inevitable occurred. The time they weighted his new bicycle down with chains and—Oh, why go on and on? The elaborate pranks she and Jason played upon Miles had been almost cruel. "Not amusing, Miles." She shook her head. "I was a holy terror."

Miles crossed his arms and gazed at her with those enigmatic silver eyes. Strange, Lara thought, she was just starting to appreciate those wonderful eyes. *Wonderful eyes?* What on earth was she going on about all of a sudden? Since when had she noticed such a personal detail of Miles Crane, let alone appreciated it?

"I envied you and Jason," Miles confessed. "You have no idea how much I wished I could have let loose sometimes and misbehaved, too."

"Somehow the picture of Miles Crane letting the air out of the police chief's tires is rather difficult to conjure."

"How do you know that I didn't consider the possibility back then?" Miles sighed. "Pranks just didn't seem to work for me, Lara, believe me. I tried once."

She was surprised. "You're kidding, Miles."

He shrugged helplessly. "Would you believe I actually put a frog in Jason's bed once?"

"I don't believe it."

He leaned his lanky frame back against the chair. "I wanted to do something adventurous and daring. I took the biggest, ugliest, dirtiest toad I could find in Aunt Lizbeth's garden and slid it right between Jason's sheets." He paused. "And do you know what happened? When it jumped onto Jason's leg, instead of being startled, he was delighted! He confessed he had been looking everywhere for his favorite frog." Miles gave a thin smile. "So I suppose you could say I learned my lesson. Certain things just don't work for me."

Miles began thinking about all the things that had never worked for him. How different matters had been for his younger brother. He had been golden. For Jason, things had always been so easy. He commanded love and received it as effortlessly as some great actors received applause. For Miles, nothing had ever come easily, and he accepted that. He remembered the Christmas Eve when Lara was sixteen. He was nearly twenty-seven then, and yet when Lara descended the staircase in a very grown-up red velvet dress that Aunt Lizbeth had given her as a special present, Miles suddenly felt eighteen years old and tongue-tied. Lara looked absolutely radiant and alive. Beautiful, in fact. Could he ever think about Christmas again without that lovely vision of Lara on the staircase? Of course, Miles remembered thinking with typical twenty-seven-year-old seriousness, that Lara was too young for him. Of course, kissing her under the mistletoe never had been even a consideration. He'd been above such childish displays of sentimental foolishness.

And then Jason had come home early from his ski vacation in Colorado, all bronzed, smiling and handsome. And apparently he was every bit as dazzled as his older brother at young Lara's unexpected transformation from a caterpillar into an exquisite butterfly. And eventually Miles found himself watching in silence as Jason gave Lara her first startled kiss under that same mistletoe. Miles remembered how he had just stood there, frozen, watching the two young people melt happily into each other's arms. It was at that moment that Miles knew with crushing finality what it meant to be on the outside looking in. He realized that fateful Christmas Eve the true meaning of being what he was. Miles Crane, the dependable. Miles Crane, the dull. Miles Crane, the man who never took chances, risks or acted on a wild impulse. How he had come to regret not having acted on his impulse to kiss Lara that Christmas Eve eight years ago. Perhaps if he had, things might have turned out differently.

Abruptly, Miles stopped himself. Who on earth was he kidding? Lara was in love with Jason. Lara

MacEuan had always been in love with Jason. Nothing Miles might have done back then would have made any difference. The outcome would have been the same. Miles chided himself. It would serve him well to remember that the only reason Lara MacEuan had agreed to come back to Pine Harbor at all was out of love for Aunt Lizbeth. He doubted very much if Lara had even thought about him during the past six years, let alone had missed him. And why should she? At this very moment, Miles Crane was painfully aware of the fact that he was a realist. And a realist always knew exactly what things he could and could not have. Unfortunately that much had not changed in the past few years.

"I'm sure that a great many things *do* work for you, Miles," Lara was saying softly. "I understand that your law firm is very successful."

Business, thought Miles ironically. Of course, business had never been a problem for him. But who on earth had been talking about business, for heaven's sake? "Yes," he agreed blandly, "business is going quite well." Wonderful. Miles gave an inward groan. His first dinner alone with Lara and this was the extent of his scintillating conversation!

"I'm glad," Lara replied with sudden uneasiness. Why did she get the impression they were both saying one thing and thinking something entirely different?

Desperately Miles reached at a conversational straw. "So, tell me. What is it like working for Hap Harrigan? Is he as funny in real life as he is on television?"

"No." Lara thought of the cadaverous, middle-aged comedian who ruled the show and his writers with an iron fist. Hap Harrigan might come across to millions of TV viewers as lovable and blundering, but in actuality he was high-strung and self-indulgent. In fact, after two years as one of Hap Harrigan's script consultants, Lara had been giving some serious thought to moving on. Sometimes being on the staff of a tyrant, no matter how successful and high-paying, was a rut in itself. A velvet-lined rut, but a rut nonetheless. Lara was now starting to consider other kinds of writing. The kinds of writing she had ignored up till now. A novel, perhaps. She paused and looked at the man who sat patiently across the table. Somehow it seemed like the most natural thing in the world to say.

"I think I'd like to write a book, Miles."

"A book?" He seemed surprised.

"Don't you think I could write a book?" she countered defensively. Oh, what made her think the man would understand, anyhow? He had never understood her. Time hadn't changed anything, apparently.

"Lara—" Miles leaned forward quickly "—of course, I think you could write a book. I'm willing to bet it would be a terrific book." He hesitated. "You just caught me off guard, that's all."

"What do you mean?"

Miles shook his head. "I'm just not used to having you confide in me."

"Oh."

"It just takes a bit of getting used to."

Lara raised an eyebrow. "Would you rather I didn't?"

"I'm glad you did, Lara." Miles gave a thin smile. "Actually it's a new experience for me. I enjoy talking to you this way." It was true. He enjoyed it immensely. It was almost as if they were two people meeting each other for the first time. On equal ground. Not only did Miles find this prospect distinctly pleasurable, but it was something that could become a habit. He liked that idea even better. His taut features softened a bit as he considered this thought.

His sudden change of expression had not been lost on Lara. For a moment, Miles looked—what should she call it? Almost tranquil. It was positively unnerving. "Miles," she murmured softly, "I wonder if—"

As if propelled by some unseen force, Miles instinctively moved closer. "You wonder if what, Lara?"

"If we should go upstairs and see your aunt now," Lara said quickly. What had she been about to say? Lara wondered in confusion. Had it been something about going outside to watch the sunset? Was *that* what she had been about to ask Miles Crane? Talk about jet lag! She just hadn't been the same person since she'd stepped off the plane.

"Oh, of course," Miles agreed hastily. "Certainly, Lara." There was the faintest tinge of disappointment in his tone—or was it Lara's imagination? "I mean, after all, that is the reason you're here."

Much to their amazement, when Lara and Miles entered the bedroom, Lizbeth Crane was sitting not in her bed, but in a comfortable wing-backed chair next to the bay window.

"Should you be sitting up, Aunt?" Miles inquired with concern. "Isn't it too soon?" He glanced critically at the nurse.

"No, Mr. Crane." The woman shook her head firmly. "It's about time. It's important for your aunt's circulation that she move about as soon as she is able."

"Now, don't be a fuddy-duddy again, Miles dear," Lizbeth shook her head irritably. "Don't give Nora a hard time."

Lara knelt down next to her godmother. "Are you feeling better, Aunt Lizbeth?"

The woman regarded her with a contented smile. "Yes, sweetheart. You don't know how wonderful it is to have you home again with us."

Lara smiled back warmly, but a faint thought was starting to trouble her. Did her godmother believe her visit was a permanent one? And was now the proper time to gently correct that impression?

"I knew you would finally get tired of all that hustle and bustle of Los Angeles. Why, they have the oddest-looking people in that town, dear," the elderly woman was saying.

Lara turned to Miles. He seemed to understand the problem. "Aunt," he began gently, "Lara is just here on a *visit*. She can only stay two weeks."

"A visit?" Lizbeth Crane looked troubled. "Only two weeks?" she echoed. There was a long pause.

"It's just that I have to be back at my job by the beginning of August, Aunt Lizbeth," Lara explained uncomfortably. The look of disappointment that clouded her godmother's face made Lara wish she had remained silent.

Lizbeth's lips tightened. "Miles, we're going to have to do something about this," she declared decisively.

"I beg your pardon, Aunt?"

"We're going to have to find a reason for Lara to stay here."

Miles exchanged a helpless glance with Lara. "What are you suggesting, Aunt?"

Now Lizbeth turned back to Lara. "Dear, don't you remember what fun you used to have here?"

Lara looked at her steadily. "Oh, yes." Sure, great fun. Like getting left at the altar on her own wedding day. A note from the groom that read, "Dear Lara, sorry, but this just isn't for me. Jason."

But Lizbeth went on, oblivious to Lara's discomfort. "The Yankee Town Fair is this very Saturday! Remember how you used to love going to that?"

"Y-yes, it was very nice," Lara stammered.

"And sailing! You used to love sailing, dear. Miles can take you on the boat tomorrow, can't you, Miles?"

"Certainly," he said, nodding. "That is, if Lara wants to go." There was a long silence.

"Lara, don't you want Miles to take you sailing?" Lizbeth inquired in a tremulous tone. "You know I can see the boat from my window. How lovely it would be to see the two of you out on the water."

Lara pursed her lips. How on earth could she refuse any request that would give her godmother such pleasure?

"Of course I want Miles to take me sailing," she agreed with a sigh. "That is, if he has the time."

"Of course he has the time," Lizbeth asserted. "Don't you, dear?"

"Oh, I certainly have the time," Miles agreed blandly.

"Then it's settled." The elderly woman appeared wistful. "How wonderful this is. Just like old times. Miles and Lara going sailing."

Lara didn't say a word. Obviously, Lizbeth Crane had become more fanciful in recent years. The truth was, Miles had never taken Lara sailing in her entire life. But if it made her godmother happy to rewrite history, then so be it. Who was Lara to argue with the blissful expression on Lizbeth Crane's withered face?

Chapter Three

The next day was Thursday, and Lara spent a quiet morning with Lizbeth. The old woman was content just to sit there in her bed and reminisce about the old days. By now, Lara was convinced that her godmother saw the past through rose-colored glasses. Miles returned home early from the office at lunchtime with the doctor in tow. Dr. Pedersen was an athletic man in his early thirties with a receding hairline and a broad smile.

"I can't get over the improvement," he murmured to Lizbeth as he returned his stethoscope to the brown leather bag. "You defy every law of medicine, Miss Crane."

"Poo." Lizbeth waved a thin arm. "I don't need a doctor to tell me that I'm feeling better. I already *know* that, silly boy!" She winked at Lara, who couldn't help smiling.

"But let's not overdo it, all right?" Dr. Pedersen murmured gently to his patient. "I don't want you to risk a relapse, so take it easy for the rest of the week."

"I want to sit out on the lawn."

"We'll discuss that in a few days," the doctor insisted with a faint smile. "If you follow my advice, there shouldn't be any problem about that, Miss Crane."

"You're too young to be a doctor," Lizbeth grumbled, but it was obvious the woman was pleased with her physician's pronouncement. Unexpectedly she then turned her attention to Miles and Lara. Miles was still dressed in a dark gray suit and Lara was clad in her jeans and sweater. "And what's the matter with you two? Why aren't you both dressed to go sailing? Those aren't sailing clothes!" she disparaged.

Out in the hallway, Lara turned to Miles. "We really shouldn't go, Miles. You have work to do, and I ought to stay with Lizbeth."

He shook his head. "My aunt has her heart set on this, Lara, and I'm not prepared to argue."

"But what about your work?" Lara protested.

Miles crossed his arms. "Do you honestly think I'd get any work done knowing that I had disappointed my great-aunt Lizbeth? And as far as your staying here with her is concerned, her nurse can do a much better job than anyone else can. Anyhow, it's what Lizbeth wants, right?"

Lara gave a reluctant nod. "I suppose so."

Miles looked at her penetratingly. "Of course, if it's the idea of my company for a few hours that you find so objectionable, that's another matter altogether."

"No, certainly not," she said hastily. "I don't feel that way at all. It's just that, well, I get the distinct impression that you have far more important matters to attend to."

Miles stared at her. "I *do*?"

"You're a busy man, Miles."

Miles pulled off his suit jacket and loosened his silk tie. "You're a busy person, too. Somehow *you* managed to find the time, Lara. As far as I'm concerned, there's nothing more important than making my great-aunt happy." He idly rolled the expensive tie in his hand. "Let me make myself quite clear. I *want* to take you sailing."

For an instant, Lara sensed the two of them were talking about something completely different. Something that had nothing to do with Aunt Lizbeth's health or the fact that they both led busy lives. Something new had been added to the equation, but Lara was reluctant to name just what it could be.

The last thing Lara thought she would be doing, when she'd received Miles's urgent phone call in California, was to go sailing on the Long Island Sound. It was a frivolity she had come completely unprepared for. She certainly hadn't thought to bring a swimsuit. However, the problem was easily resolved when she discovered that the bottom two drawers in the bureau of the guest bedroom were still filled with neatly folded stacks of Lara's old summer clothes. As she sorted through the pile of T-shirts and cotton shorts, Lara realized more than ever that her godmother had never given up hope of her return. There was something very poignant about the handsewn satin sachets filled with lavender that lay interspersed with Lara's clothes. Just another loving and sensitive touch of Lizbeth Crane, she thought.

Ten minutes later, Lara stared at her reflection in the floor-length oval mirror. Although her body had matured since high school, she still managed to fit into her favorite old bathing suit. The slightly faded red-and-white striped maillot clung to every curve and was cut high up on the leg. It showed off Lara's California tan to perfection. Somehow, though, she was grateful for her old pair of matching red shorts. It made the swimsuit feel a bit less revealing. Odd that she should feel that way, Lara thought, tying a red ribbon around her ponytail. After all, it had never particularly bothered her six years ago to wear such skimpy attire. And on the beach in Los Angeles, Lara had worn her share of the trendiest string bikinis. But somehow, today was different. For reasons she could not explain, Lara felt strangely self-conscious about the prospect of wearing the scanty swimwear in front of Miles. Perhaps it had to do with the fact that the man always seemed so proper. In any case, she was ill at ease with the entire situation. And as far as her

swimming attire, well, Lara shrugged philosophi-
cally, she would simply have to make do with what she
had.

Miles was waiting for her at the bottom of the staircase. He looked her over briefly, and remarked, "I
remember that outfit, Lara."

"You're kidding."

"Why would I kid about something like that?" He
gestured at the ponytail. "I remember that, too."

Lara quirked an eyebrow. It never occurred to her
that Miles had taken note one way or the other of the
type of clothing she wore, or the most minute details
of her hairstyle. Especially all those years ago. Looking at her companion now, Lara recognized nothing
familiar about his sailing attire. She could not remember Miles Crane having been dressed so casually.
He looked disturbingly vital and masculine. Those
were two words that had never come to mind when she
thought of Miles Crane. But here he stood, definitely
and disturbingly male, in a navy blue polo shirt and
faded khaki shorts. He wore a pair of scuffed, old
sneakers, and an expensive pair of sunglasses hung
from a cord around his neck.

"Have I rendered you speechless, Lara?" Miles
murmured in faint surprise.

"Certainly not!" she retorted, unaware of the two
bright spots of color that suffused her cheeks.

Lord above, Miles realized in amazement. Had he
actually caused Lara MacEuan to blush? What strange
new world was this? In the past twenty-four hours,

since picking Lara up at the airport, Miles had begun to recognize the existence of brand-new possibilities. Wonderful, previously unheard-of possibilities. He took a step backward and almost collided with the ice cooler he had recently filled with beverage cans and sandwiches. "Uh, we'd better get going." Inwardly Miles sighed. He might have graduated first in his class at law school, and he might have the most successful legal practice in town, but Lara MacEuan still had the uncanny ability to make him feel like a bumbling schoolboy. With an assumed air of confidence, Miles put on his brand-new designer sunglasses. He hoped they would make him look dashing and sophisticated. Instead, the glasses immediately slid off the bridge of his nose and smacked him sharply in the mouth.

"Are you okay, Miles?" Lara looked at him with concern.

"Just fine," he muttered, quickly tucking the lenses into his shirt pocket. Well, he thought deprecatingly, enough for assuming a sophisticated and dashing air. He had certainly been right yesterday about things never coming easily for him. Embarrassed, he cleared his throat and tried to glance purposefully at his gold wristwatch. "We'd better get going."

"Of course." Lara nodded.

"According to the marine forecast, the next few hours should be perfect for sailing."

"I'm sure you're right," she agreed, looking after him in bewilderment as Miles strode confidently toward the front door.

And promptly tripped on one of his own shoelaces.

It *was* the perfect weather for sailing. Already a line of sails billowed along the distant horizon. The marina at Pine Harbor hosted no more than one hundred craft, some of them elaborate racing yachts, some smaller powerboats and others the simplest of sailboats. It had been six years since Lara was at the Pine Harbor Community Yacht Club. It was where generations of MacEuans and Cranes had moored their various boats over the years. It was said that the sea was in their blood. She twisted her mouth and looked onto the Long Island Sound from the aging, slightly rickety pier. How often had she stood here at the edge of this very same pier, waving goodbye to her parents as they set sail on *Trade Winds* for yet another exotic port of call. A port of call that was certain to be alluring and adventurous, but definitely did not include Lara. She often wondered, after years of feeling left out of her parents' travels, if Willy and Denise somehow knew that their only child simply had not inherited the family love of the sea. Maybe that was the reason they never took Lara with them. Or maybe the answer was far simpler. Her parents didn't want Lara along in their own private world. There was a lonely ache for the natural bond with a mother and father that had somehow never developed in Lara's case.

She pushed the unhappy thought away from her mind. There was no use crying over spilled milk. Things were the way they were and no one could change them. Why go on about it? Hastily, she looked over at Miles. "Which boat are we taking today?" As far as she could remember, the Cranes owned a variety, always adding and subtracting from their tiny flotilla.

He hesitated, then assisted her onto the small dinghy that would take them out to the mooring. "I thought we'd go on one of the older craft." He waited till Lara had steadied herself in the tiny boat and began to row with powerful, sure strokes away from the dock.

"Which one?" Lara repeated curiously. Was Miles being deliberately evasive? she wondered. At the same time, she couldn't help but notice the muscular strength of Miles's forearms beneath his golden tanned skin as he continued to pull the oars with practiced precision. Had there really been a time when she considered the man to be little more than a listless string-bean?

"Over there," Miles was saying now.

Lara followed the direction of his glance to where a pale blue-and-white sailing craft was moored. It was achingly familiar, with its distinctive mahogany brightwork and bow design. "Oh," was all she could manage to say for a moment.

It was *Lara's Smile*, the twenty-three-foot sailboat her grandfather had commissioned on the day she was born. Lizbeth Crane had later told her, in the same tone one tells a child a fairy tale, that the old man had taken one look at his newborn grandchild's tiny up-turned mouth through the windows of the maternity ward nursery and had been instantly enchanted. Hence the name of the boat. As Miles drew the dinghy closer, Lara could easily recognize the familiar words painted in elaborate gold script across the stern. *Lara's Smile.* Odd, she thought. Except for that initial pang of nostalgia, why did the sight of this lovely old fiberglass sloop leave her curiously unmoved? Perhaps because it represented a part of her past that was truly devoid of real love or sentiment. In fact, Lara was surprised to see the boat here at all. She had somehow assumed that *Lara's Smile*, along with the old MacEuan house and property, had been sold off by her parents several years back. While Willy MacEuan may have inherited a love for the sea, certainly he had not inherited his family's business acumen. Ultimately most of the MacEuan fortune had dissipated.

"Did *you* buy this boat?" She looked at Miles in bewilderment.

He gave a terse nod and pulled the dinghy along-side the sloop, lifting the oars out of the water and stowing them securely aboard. "Watch your step," he said as he assisted Lara out of the tiny boat and onto the larger vessel.

"Why did you buy it, Miles?" Lara was completely baffled. It simply made no sense.

Miles busied himself with unlocking the hatch and pulling out the long vinyl cushions that fit along the roomy cockpit. "What does it matter?" He finally turned to face her.

"Oh, it matters." Lara met his glance head-on. Yes, oddly enough, it *did* matter.

"Why?" It was Miles's turn to ask.

"You must own half-a-dozen boats already."

"So, what's one more?" Miles tried to sound casual.

To Lara's newly sensitized ears, Miles's words didn't quite ring true. "Why did you buy *Lara's Smile*?" she repeated quietly.

He eyed her steadily. "Lara, they just don't make boats like this any more. You're forgetting that fiberglass was still a new idea back in the midsixties. Like so many of the early models, *Lara's Smile* is a solid piece of workmanship. Super-rigid, overweight and overengineered. After all, they were still learning about the new material back then...."

"I never thought of that." Lara seemed convinced by his explanation. She should have known that Miles had a practical reason for everything he did. What had she believed for just a moment? That Miles might have actually been motivated by pure sentiment? What an absolutely absurd notion!

Miles regarded her in silence. Apparently Lara had accepted the explanation. Good, he thought with satisfaction. The last thing he wanted her to know was his true reason for purchasing the twenty-four-year-old sloop. The real reason, of course, was extremely sentimental. Highly personal. One of a few genuinely impulsive gestures in Miles's entire life. It was the bankruptcy auction for the MacEuan estate. The bidding for *Lara's Smile* had started low and really wasn't going anywhere. The fact was, although it was a lovely vessel, there was nothing particularly exceptional about it, especially to a well-heeled leisure sailor who could have his pick of an already glutted marketplace. And when a stranger from out of the state was going to buy the sloop for what seemed like a song, Miles knew he simply could not permit such a thing to happen. It was Lara's namesake.

As Lara watched Miles climb up along the rigging, she was struck with the man's agility. In a few minutes, the sails were billowing in the summer wind. She silently observed her companion as he maneuvered himself surefootedly along the edge of the boat, handling the lines with impressive skill. Miles was in his element on the water.

"Lara," he said, motioning behind her, "would you like to take the tiller?"

"Sure," she replied, and reached for the polished mahogany handle that controlled the steering.

It had been years, but maybe it was like riding a bicycle, Lara mused as she guided the boat out of the small channel and into the wide expanse of the Long Island Sound. A person never forgets how to sail. Miles leaned back against the cushions and studied Lara silently.

"Would you like a soda or a sandwich?"

"No thanks." She paused. "Any place in particular you'd like to go?" To one side of them were the beaches of southern Connecticut. Off in the distance lay the shoreline of Long Island.

"Oh, it doesn't matter." As far as Miles was concerned, it was extremely pleasant just drifting along with his beautiful companion. How often he had fantasized about a day such as this one. A balmy July afternoon, the sparkling silver of the water, and Lara MacEuan alone with him in a sailboat on the Sound. What more could any man ask for? He must remember to thank Aunt Lizbeth for inadvertently making such an unlikely scenario become a reality.

Lara continued to steer the sloop expertly through the rolling water, occasionally glancing over at Miles. There was an expression on his face that she could never remember having seen before. What could one call it? Almost a look of serenity. *Serenity.* Now there was another word that had never previously come to mind when one thought of Miles. Strange. Lara was now beginning to recognize other attributes of her companion. Had he always been so fit and athletic? Why hadn't she ever noticed before?

For the next couple of hours, they drifted along the relatively peaceful body of water in near silence. They were lulled into such tranquility that there was no need to speak at all. Lara was completely relaxed for the first time in ages, filled with a feeling of warmth and well-being. And it was obvious that Miles was similarly affected.

At one point he said, "Take a look at the clouds, Lara."

She followed his gaze upward. The varied and beautiful shapes of white streaked their way across the deep blue of the July sky. She couldn't help but recall with a smile how Lizbeth had always encouraged them to let their imaginations give names to all the different shapes of clouds. "That one looks just like a rocking horse." Lara pointed at one fluffy apparition.

"And I'd say the one over there is definitely a dachshund." Miles gestured at a long, stringy white wisp.

"You're right." Lara grinned. It really did resemble the short, stumpy but lovable canine.

"Of course I'm right." Miles grinned back.

Lara lapsed into silence again. The last thing she ever thought she might be doing on a day like this was sitting comfortably with Miles and talking about clouds. How had it suddenly become so easy to be with this man and enjoy his company? Rather belatedly it occurred to Lara that she was having quite a wonderful time. Alone with Miles. More disturbingly, Lara was reluctant for the afternoon to come to an end.

"Is something the matter?" Miles inquired with a curious quirk of his eyebrow.

"No, not at all!" Lara answered hastily. *You bet something is the matter, Mr. Miles Crane! After twenty-four years of considering you to be the dul-*

lest, most boring man on the face of the earth, I suddenly discover something totally incredible: you're fun to be with!

Miles was mystified. Just a moment ago, Lara seemed to be so happy, as if she was actually having a good time in his company. It had made him feel delightful. Almost cocky. As if for the first time, he had stepped out from behind his younger brother's shadow. As if for the first time, Lara was regarding him as a living, breathing man, instead of a shadowy reflection of Jason. "Are you ready to go back, now?" The words were out of his mouth before he could stop them. Miles could hardly believe he was so ready to concede defeat.

Lara looked at him in surprise. She hadn't realized that Miles was bored and couldn't wait to get home. Until this moment, she had actually been convinced that her companion was enjoying the afternoon as much as she was. Well, she was wrong. "Sure, Miles," she replied uncomfortably. "Whatever you want to do."

What Miles really wanted to do was sail the sloop over toward one of the tiny islands that dotted this part of the Sound. He wanted to drop anchor and swim over to the rocky, narrow beach with Lara. And then the two of them could just lie on their backs and conjure up more imaginative visions of clouds. *That* was what he really wanted to do.

"Should I turn back now, Miles?" Lara tried not to let the disappointment show in her voice.

"Wait a minute," Miles said impulsively. "Why don't we sail over to Minawin Island and take a swim?"

"Sounds like fun," came Lara's unexpected reply.

Miles was filled with a feeling of triumph. Maybe sometimes, things *did* come easily. Perhaps someone "up there" liked him. Whatever the reason, Miles couldn't help smiling. Lara was enjoying the day with him, and she was apparently in no hurry to get home.

They dropped anchor in four feet of water. Minawin Island, with its thin strip of sand and scrubby trees, lay one hundred yards in the distance. There were no other boats in sight.

"Race you to the beach!" Lara challenged, as she pulled off her red shorts and stood ready to go over the side.

"Sure," Miles murmured, unable to take his eyes off her curvy body. The last time he remembered seeing Lara in that same striped bathing suit, she had been a skinny schoolgirl. Now, the high cut legs of the faded maillot served only to accentuate how sweetly her body had matured. With an effort, Miles hastily pushed the enticing thought from his mind, and turned away from Lara with reluctance. He removed his own polo shirt and khaki shorts to reveal a pair of loose-fitting navy swim trunks. "Ready," he said to his companion, and without another word, they slipped carefully over the side.

At first, Lara matched Miles stroke for stroke, but she was unable to keep up with his powerful body as he knifed through the water. To Lara, Miles resembled an arrow shooting straight and sure toward its target. She couldn't help giving a murmur of admiration as she joined him, wet and dripping, on the small beach.

"You beat me fair and square, Miles. I must admit."

Miles leaned over on his side and regarded her intently. "Yes, I did. Fair and square." The water ran in rivulets down the taut muscles of his tanned chest.

Lara tried to ignore this disturbing awareness by retorting blithely, "Of course, you had the advantage."

"I did?" Miles, in turn, was preoccupied with his delightful appreciation of Lara's supple figure beneath the wet, clinging maillot. "How did I have the advantage, Lara?" He idly reached out his hand to touch a wayward strand of her brown hair that had escaped from its ponytail. Almost unaware of his actions, Miles gently brushed the wet strand away from her face.

"The reason you have the advantage—" Lara found herself suddenly stammering at his touch "—is because you're a man."

"I'm a man. Well, that's certainly news," Miles said teasingly, and continued to stroke Lara's smooth hair.

"What I . . . what I mean is, well—" Lara actually felt a shiver when Miles's fingers brushed against the nape of her neck "—uh, that is, a man has the advantage because he is traditionally taller and stronger."

"Is that so?" Miles's breath fanned her moist cheek.

Lara suppressed a quiver as she savored the unexpectedly tantalizing closeness. "So maybe the race wasn't exactly fair and square, after all." His voice came out slightly high.

"Thing seldom are fair." Miles's mouth hovered scant inches above her own.

For one dizzying instant, Lara thought he was about to kiss her. "Miles, I—"

"You *what*, Lara?" he whispered hoarsely, his lips continuing their slow, inevitable descent.

He was going to kiss her, Lara realized with delicious anticipation. Any moment now, that hard firm mouth would capture her own and she would finally know what it would be like to be kissed by Miles Crane. Involuntarily, her lips parted slightly to meet his.

"Ahoy, there!" A booming voice shattered the idyll in an instant. It was followed by a chorus of catcalls and cheers.

"What the—" Miles and Lara looked up, startled. So absorbed had the two of them been in their tender moment that they had completely failed to notice the appearance of a flashy powerboat filled with half-a-dozen rowdy high school students. They had moored alongside *Lara's Smile* and begun jumping into the water completely clothed, still holding bottles of beer.

Several of the girls gave high-pitched squeals of protest as one of the young men began pouring the contents of his beer bottle over their heads.

Miles and Lara exchanged disapproving glances. Both had always found such reckless behavior on the water to be outrageously irresponsible, let alone very dangerous.

"I suppose this is our cue to leave, Lara," Miles remarked with distaste. Damn, he thought irritably. Talk about bad timing! Just when he'd come close to finally kissing Lara the way he'd meant to all those years ago. Had it been his imagination, or had she actually seemed to welcome the prospect? The thought of Lara's lips lifting eagerly to meet his own was enough to drive Miles to distraction. Who knows what might have happened, he continued to imagine wildly, if the two of them hadn't been interrupted by those high school delinquents!

"I suppose you're right," Lara agreed reluctantly, as the hoots and screams from the unruly teenagers grew even louder. She followed Miles back to the water's edge, feeling oddly disappointed. She couldn't believe her mad tumult of emotions. For a moment, Lara realized that she really had wanted Miles to kiss her. She cleared her throat quickly. Of course, the moment was gone, as if it had never existed. Perhaps it was better that way. The last thing she needed, Lara decided, was to be any more confused about her feelings than she already was.

"Ready?" Miles asked briefly.

"Ready." Lara nodded with affected casualness, and then the two of them swam purposefully back to the boat, making sure to give the noisy revelers a wide berth.

The two of them scarcely exchanged a word on the trip back to the marina. Miles took the tiller and seemed lost in his own thoughts. He seemed almost like his old self, quiet and uncommunicative.

Miles was fighting for self-control. He desperately needed to stabilize his emotions. The last thing he wanted right now was for Lara to see through his cool facade. He didn't want her to know how terribly vulnerable he was. It was far too risky. The magical air of confidence he had possessed on the island somehow managed to elude him now. Out of the corner of his eye, he watched as Lara sat pensively gazing at the shoreline. Was she admiring the postcard look of Pine Harbor in the distance, with its green trees, rolling hills and old homes. Or perhaps she was imagining the shapes of dragons and unicorns in the thick, fleecy clouds.

Half an hour later, *Lara's Smile* was guided gently back to its mooring. The sails were taken down and the gear neatly stowed inside the cabin. When the dinghy had almost completed its brief trip back to the dock, Lara finally looked at him. "Thank you, Miles," she said simply.

"For what?"

She stared at him steadily. "For taking me sailing today."

"It's really not necessary to thank me, Lara. I'd do anything for Aunt Lizbeth."

"Oh, of course," she answered quickly.

Miles flinched. What on earth had caused him to make such an offhand remark? Was it because he had been fighting every impulse to say what was really on his mind? Which was, of course, that Lara never had to thank him for anything, especially when it involved spending time with her. But seeing those rowdy teenage boaters had brought back more unpleasant memories for Miles. He was remembering the first time he had seen Lara in that sexy little red-and-white striped bathing suit, her hair, which was so much longer then, had been pulled back into the familiar ponytail. She couldn't have been more than seventeen years old, and Jason had taken her out on his high performance speedboat. He had been more than just reckless or daring. Jason had had several drinks before leaving the yacht club and picking up Lara at the dock. With Lara sitting in the seat beside him, he had pushed the powerboat to speeds unsafe for the choppy waves of the Sound that day. Worst of all, he had nearly collided with a small catamaran loaded with several young children. Miles had angrily sailed off to confront his younger brother. Miles had been positively livid. Later, Miles had recalled the look of astonishment on Lara's face. It was one of the few times she had ever seen him lose his temper. For a long time afterward, Miles had imagined that Lara seemed to be just slightly afraid of him. That thought had bothered him greatly. But there had been nothing to do or say to change that.

Miles stepped up onto the dock and reached out his hand to assist Lara. Wordlessly she jumped up alongside him on the rickety old pier, and the two of them began to walk back toward the parking area. Suddenly a loose piece of rotting wood got caught in her sneaker tread and sent her flying toward the ground.

"I've got you!" Miles caught her as she stumbled and managed to break what might have otherwise been a nasty fall. For just a moment, he held her tightly against his chest, his strong arms clasped about her slender waist. "I've got you, Lara," he repeated in a near whisper. But he didn't release his hold.

"Thank..." she began to murmur, but the words died in her throat. It was delicious to be held in Miles's arms at last, to feel his heart thudding against her ear. And he was actually trembling, Lara marveled. Against her own volition, she relaxed her body even more to enjoy the intimate contact.

"Lara!" Miles exclaimed hoarsely against her hair.

"What?" she asked with a sigh against the soft cotton material of his navy blue polo shirt.

"Lara, I—" he began urgently, then stopped himself. Miles pulled back from the unexpected embrace and stared down at her.

"What?" she repeated gently. "What did you want to say, Miles?"

For a moment, he seemed incapable of speech. Then his common sense took over. "I was just thinking that it's nearly time for dinner," Miles said abruptly, "and we certainly don't want to be late."

"Right." Lara nodded slowly. Inside, she was a jumble of confused nerves. Nothing had ever felt so right as when Miles had held her against his hard body. How utterly unexpected. How unbelievably strange. But the strangest thing of all, Lara suddenly realized, was that in all the time she had spent with Miles today, she had never once given the slightest thought to Jason Crane.

Chapter Four

The next few days passed quickly enough, and Lizbeth Crane seemed to grow stronger and healthier at an almost miraculous rate. Her doctor credited her remarkable constitution, but Miles was convinced that the true answer lay elsewhere. Lara MacEuan, the proxy child of Lizbeth's lonely world, had returned home, and the elderly woman's life had purpose and direction once again.

Even though neither Lara nor Miles ever mentioned the disturbing incident on the pier, the moment remained in her memory like a burning ember. Lara's bewilderment knew no bounds. She had spent the past six years haunted by her ill-fated love for Jason Crane. In Los Angeles, she had never let another man come that close to her. And it ran deeper than that. Lara had simply never again shown interest in another man. Oh, there had been some members of the opposite sex whom she met socially or through her many show business contacts. Many were successful, attractive, vigorous men who complained that Lara would never let them near enough to even hold their hands. They ultimately would give up in exasperation and call her names such as "frigid" and a "cold fish," but Lara could not have cared less. It was as if she had lived the past six years of her life inside some kind of bubble. Every man she had met always fell short in comparison to Jason. Despite his betrayal, no one could ever compare to his looks, his vitality and his sheer dynamic personality.

Lara had been convinced that this trip to Pine Harbor would open up a hornet's nest of painful memories, and instead, those memories now seemed oddly distant. Almost as if they were someone else's memories and not her own.

What had happened, anyhow? Lara's lips compressed in a tight smile. The answer was two words—Miles Crane. In a single afternoon, he had turned her life upside down. The entire revelation made Lara extremely uncomfortable. Now, an element of uncertainty and suspense hovered in the air. Gone were the past six years of bland, numb nothingness that had served as a secure, impenetrable sanctuary for her wounded heart. Lara had become accustomed to controlling every aspect of her personal world, and now, events seemed to be spinning at a dizzy pace, acquiring a life of their own.

One example was the idea fixed firmly in Lizbeth Crane's mind that her great-nephew and goddaughter should go to the Yankee Town Fair. Miles, who had been strangely silent and uncommunicative since the unexpected embrace at the dock, now seemed eager to please his aunt.

"Of course, I'd be happy to escort Lara to the fair." He nodded matter-of-factly, and turned toward her. "Is that all right with you, Lara?"

She regarded him quizzically for a moment, trying to detect the slightest trace of emotion or tension, but there was neither. "Sure, Miles," she replied with studied blandness. "That sounds just fine." Well, Lara shrugged to herself, maybe she had overreacted to the events of that previous day. After all, how much experience had she had with men recently? Surely she had placed too much importance on a simple gesture of affection both on Minawin Island and later on the pier. That had to be it, Lara resolved finally. She felt positively foolish for having made such a big deal over a simple caress and casual hug. How silly she was.

"And I'd love for you to wear that pretty pink dress," Lizbeth was saying now.

"I beg your pardon, Auntie?" Lara was jolted back to reality.

"That pink sundress hanging in your closet, dear," her godmother declared emphatically. "I bought it for you in St. Thomas four, or was it five, years ago. How pretty it will look with your coloring!''

"Oh, how very thoughtful of you, Auntie.'' Lara felt positively embarrassed. While she had spent years wiping the existence of the entire Crane family from her mind, this sweet, caring woman had never stopped thinking of her. Planning for her happiness. Buying her gifts. Keeping her room in readiness just in case she should ever return. Lara felt quite humbled. She took a look inside herself and realized the full extent of her own selfishness. "Thank you very much,'' she said, then kissed Lizbeth's wrinkled cheek affectionately. "It's a lovely dress. Of course, I'll wear it.''

Miles gave her an approving nod from the other side of the room as if to say Lara had done just the right thing. In an odd way, she found this slightly annoying. After all, Lara was not putting on a performance for Lizbeth Crane's benefit. She was being completely sincere.

"And the two of you remember,'' Lizbeth was saying, "you'll be representing the family, so be on your best behavior!''

"Right, Aunt.'' Miles nodded with mock solemnity. "Our best behavior.''

"Don't worry,'' Lara said reassuringly, "I'll keep a close watch on Miles and make sure he doesn't get out of line.''

"Is that so?'' Miles said softly, a strange expression on his face.

"Absolutely," she tossed back lightly, trying to ignore the fact that her stomach was starting to turn somersaults from the way Miles was suddenly looking at her.

"How exactly did you intend to keep a close watch on me, Lara?" Miles probed insistently, an alien glitter in his silver eyes.

"I suppose I'll just have to stick to you like glue, Miles Crane," she remarked blithely.

"I think I'd like that." His gaze locked with hers. "I think I'd like it a lot, Lara."

"You would, hmm?" She attempted to sound flip, but her voice shook ever so slightly.

This interesting little exchange did not go unnoticed by Lizbeth Crane, who watched, listened and decoded the messages transmitted by two pairs of eyes and the faintest of tremors in two separate voices. At first, Lizbeth registered utter astonishment. This was a revelation. It was a new development as welcome as it was unexpected. The seeds of a secret hope had been planted, and a broad, knowing smile began to spread like rays of sunlight within Lizbeth's heart. But aloud she declared with mock indignation, "Are the two of you going to just stand there, or are you going to put on your nice clothes and go to the fair? It's bad enough that I am unable to attend festivities that I have not missed since the year I was born!" And just for calculated effect, she added with the weariest sigh in her repertoire, "I'm getting so tired...."

"Are you all right, Auntie?" Both Lara and Miles looked at her in concern.

"Oh, I'll be fine once I get some rest, I suppose." Lizbeth's eyelids fluttered dramatically. "But first, it would be so lovely if I could see how the two of you look in your going-out clothes."

"Oh, of course," Lara agreed hastily.

"Yes, Aunt," Miles chimed in quickly. "We'll both go and change right away. Won't we, Lara?"

"Right away." Lara nodded her assent.

"I ... I don't want to be any trouble," Lizbeth said weakly. "I ... understand if either of you had made other plans—"

"It's no trouble," Lara asserted.

"No trouble at all," Miles echoed.

Lizbeth watched silently as her great-nephew and goddaughter left her room to get dressed. As soon as they disappeared down the hallway, she chuckled to herself in delight.

The Yankee Town Fair was held every July on the village green, which overlooked the Long Island Sound from a high vantage point above the marina. The fair was an annual celebration to commemorate an important event in early American history. Members of the local historical society dressed in period costumes to reenact the event. Booths with home-baked pies, cakes and other treats were set up. Traditional crafts were proudly displayed for sale, and the community band played in the white, gingerbread-trimmed wood gazebo in the center of the town square. The fair had been a part of Lara's childhood, and marked a time of particularly happy memories.

Now, standing before the oval mahogany mirror in the guest bedroom, she surveyed her own reflection with a critical eye. The pink sundress, with its halter-cut top and tight-fitting waist, was made of a fine quality, soft cotton. It flattered her figure, ending just above the knee. The weather was far too hot and humid for stockings, Lara though as she slid her bare, tanned legs into a pair of flat, white summer sandals. With a final brush to her loose brown hair, parting it to one side, she was ready to go. Lara paused for a minute, and after the briefest consideration, reached for her makeup case. She hadn't worn anything on her face since the day she'd arrived. Suddenly Lara felt the need to look as attractive as possible. Of course it had nothing to do with Miles, she thought hastily, and applied a faint blusher to her cheeks and just a touch of mascara to her already long eyelashes. No, not at all. Lara reached for a tube of pink lip gloss. It was simply that she wanted to look her best when she ran into all her old friends in town, she convinced herself.

A few minutes later, she stood with Miles at the foot of Lizbeth's bed as they both submitted themselves for the woman's approval. Miles had changed into a dark beige polo shirt and matching olive khaki slacks. The brown leather belt he wore accentuated the fact that the man had no excess fat on his taut waist. Lara observed him out of the corner of her eye, aware that those recent disturbing thoughts about Miles Crane were once more starting to surface. The man was in superb physical shape, there was no doubt about it. It was impossible to ignore the fact that while Miles might not possess his younger brother's hulking physique, the older Crane had a definite allure all his own. He was the substance without the flash, Lara marveled to herself.

"The dress is lovely," Lizbeth was gushing now. "Don't you think so, Miles, dear?"

"Lovely," Miles murmured softly, his silver gaze traveling over Lara from head to toe.

"Thanks," she responded with a casualness she did not feel. "You look very nice yourself, Miles."

Miles gave a brief nod of acknowledgment, but it was clear that he felt Lara was merely being polite.

"You know, Lara," Lizbeth began, filling the conversational void, "I was just thinking that while your outfit is rather stunning, it is somewhat lacking in ornamentation."

"I beg your pardon, Auntie?" Lara pulled away from Miles's intense stare with a small degree of relief. "What did you say?"

"I was saying," the elderly woman said with a smile, "that your dress is very pretty, but it still needs something." She gestured toward a tiny box on the vanity table. "Open that up, dear."

Questioningly, Lara walked over to the bedside table and picked up the box. It was faded cardboard, tied with a distinctly brand-new pink ribbon. Inside, lying against a square of gauze, was a small, oval-shaped locket on a delicate filigree chain. "Oh, it's beautiful," Lara exclaimed.

"I was hoping you'd like it." Lizbeth seemed pleased. "I'd been meaning to give it to you for the longest time, Lara. Look inside, dear."

Lara pressed the tiny spring and the locket opened to reveal a miniature photograph of an old three-masted schooner. "*The Mermaid*!" Lara smiled. She would know that ship anywhere. It was Torquil MacEuan's pride and joy, the hearty sailing vessel that had been the cornerstone of the MacEuan fortune. "Where did you ever find this, Auntie?" she asked.

Lizbeth's bright blue gaze softened. "Your great-uncle Rory gave it to me as an engagement present."

"Oh!" Lara was concerned. "I couldn't take this from you, Auntie. It means too much to you."

Lizbeth shook her head determinedly. "I always meant to give it to my daughter, Lara. But since—" she stopped for a moment. "I can think of no one I would rather give it to than my only godchild. Particularly, a godchild who also happens to be a MacEuan."

"Oh, Auntie." Lara was deeply touched. There was no way for her to refuse such a precious gift, or even a logical reason why she should.

But Lizbeth wasn't paying attention at the moment. Instead, she was remembering Rory, her one and only love who had drowned so tragically before their wedding could take place. How much Lara resembled her dead fiancé, Lizbeth was thinking. The same hazel eyes, the same smile, and most of all, the same gentle, caring heart. It was a belief far too personal to ever confide to anyone else, but Lizbeth was convinced that Rory lived on in Lara. This is what their daughter would have been like, the old woman knew in her heart. It was one of the reasons she had always been so devoted to Lara.

Lizbeth Crane forced herself back to the present. She could not change the events of the past, but it was certainly within her power to try to control the future. No one had ever realized the depth of Lizbeth's anguish when Jason, her favorite nephew, had so callously and unexpectedly jilted Lara on their wedding day. But time had a way of soothing painful memories, and now, watching Miles and Lara standing in front of her, Lizbeth was aware of other alternatives. Of course, sometimes, things didn't come so easy. Young people often didn't recognize what was staring them head-on, as plain as the noses on their faces. A helpful push by an interested third party might be all that was required to get the ball rolling.

"Miles." She looked over at her nephew, who had been watching silently from the other side of the bed. "Come over here and help Lara put on the locket."

"Oh, that's not necessary, Auntie," Lara blurted out. "I can do it myself."

"Nonsense, the clasp is tricky." Lizbeth waved her hand in a gesture that brooked no refusals. "Miles, go over and help Lara with the locket. You're so good at those silly mechanical things.''

"Of course, Aunt," Miles said evenly, and strode over to the other side of the bed. "Let's take a look at it, shall we?" he said to Lara.

She held out her hand, and he removed the locket from her warm palm, examining the clasp with a critical eye. "It looks simple enough," he remarked blandly, and paused. "Um, I think it would be easier if you lifted your hair out of the way for a minute. I wouldn't want any strands to get caught in the clasp."

Without a word, Lara swept the glossy brown strands up away from her nape and stood there, holding her hair on the top of her head. Deftly, Miles stood behind her and drew the necklace around her throat. For an instant, Lara felt his hard fingers linger on her bare skin, and his cool breath against the back of her neck, as he fastened the locket.

"There," Miles said in a curiously unsteady voice. "That ought to do it."

"Thank you," Lara said quickly. The color tinting her cheeks all of a sudden did not come from her cosmetic blusher.

Lizbeth smiled in satisfaction. "Oh, it looks wonderful on you, dear. Just as I knew it would." An awkward silence hung in the air, and the elderly woman added hastily, "Oh, but I'm keeping the two of you and you'll be late for the festivities!" She waved her hand. "Go, shoo, already! Have a lovely time! Send everyone my regards!"

The fair was in full swing when the two of them arrived at the grassy park. The Pine Harbor High School drill team was entertaining the crowds with a dazzling display of baton twirling. One baton flew up so high it became tangled in the power lines, and electricity for the entire town was temporarily shut off. The community band was playing a cheerfully off-key version of "Yankee Doodle," and old acquaintances whom Lara hadn't seen in years constantly rushed up to greet her.

"Lara MacEuan, as I live and breathe," declared Mona Jackson. "Is that really you?" In high school, Mona had been the blond, skinny captain of their cheerleading squad. She was still blond but no longer skinny. Self-consciously the woman glanced down at her stomach. "Oh, yeah. Can you believe it, Lara? It's my third!"

Lara shook her head in amazement. "Congratulations," was all she could think to say.

"Lara, my gosh! Has it been six years?" boomed the voice of Chubby Winslow, the president of their senior class. "How ya doin', Miles?" He grinned. Chubby had been the most good-natured human being Lara ever knew. His parents had owned the local coffee shop, but Chubby had always dreamed of being a nightclub comedian.

"It's good to see you, Chubs." Lara gave a genuine smile. "How have you been?"

"Terrific, but, hey! Not as good as you. Say," he said, leaning forward with a wink. "You're a big

Hollywood writer, now. Think you could put in a good word for me?''

''Sure, Chubs. Did you want me to talk to someone about an audition?'' she responded tentatively.

''He's just kidding.'' Miles twisted his mouth.

''Ah, c'mon, Miles. Don't be a killjoy,'' the plump young man groaned. ''This could be my big break!''

Miles crossed his arms and his smile broadened. ''What Chubby has neglected to tell you, Lara, is that he's currently in his third year at Yale Medical School.''

''You're kidding!'' Lara's eyes widened in amazement.

Chubby gave a reluctant shrug. ''Yeah, isn't that a pip?''

''Why, how wonderful, Chubs!''

''He's going to be a neurosurgeon,'' Miles revealed matter-of-factly.

''Only because I got this scholarship, see,'' Chubby explained. ''Otherwise, I would have headed straight to Vegas after college. Show business is in my blood, Lara.''

''Chubs Winslow, a brain surgeon!'' Lara mused to Miles later on. ''Who ever would have thought such a thing?''

''I suppose one never knows how a person is going to turn out,'' Miles remarked vaguely.

''I suppose not.''

No, Lara was thinking. One never did know how much a person could change in a few years. Miles, for example. He seemed so much more alive and confident. Before, Lara had always considered him to be so nondescript. So completely lacking in any masculine appeal. But that was years ago, and today, all Lara could think of was how the nape of her neck still tingled from when he had fastened her locket.

The afternoon passed quite pleasantly. While Lara was constantly deluged with surprised greetings from childhood companions, it was interesting to notice how very popular Miles had become in Pine Harbor. While it might be true that the Cranes had always been the wealthiest, most influential family in town, it was quite clear that Miles Crane was well-liked and respected in his own right.

"Hi, Miles," a distinctly feminine voice murmured.

"Oh, Caroline." Miles gave a warm smile to the rather attractive red-haired young woman dressed in an extremely flattering white linen pantsuit. "Lara." Miles turned to her briefly. "I'd like you to meet one of the new associates at my firm, Caroline Sinclair."

"I'm delighted to meet you." Lara gave the pretty lawyer her brightest smile and extended her hand.

"Same here." The other woman's perfectly manicured hand was cold and her cordial tone seemed slightly assumed. Caroline immediately turned her attention back to Miles. "I was hoping we could get together and discuss the Johnson deposition." She paused. "You've been very hard to get a hold of these past few days."

"I know," Miles was saying apologetically. "Family matters have been taking up a good deal of my time."

"Oh, of course." Caroline nodded sympathetically. "How is your dear aunt?"

"Much better." Miles glanced briefly at Lara, who had already begun to feel invisible. It was an uncomfortable and unique situation. Lara had never felt left out before in her life. She didn't care for it one bit, and she certainly did not care for the way the woman was positively gushing over Miles.

"Lizbeth is such a darling, sweet person. I must come up to the house again soon and visit her," Caroline was saying.

Again? Soon? Lara's mind was a jolt of indignant confusion. How often did this flirtatious little hussy enjoy the hospitality of the Crane home? More important, how often did the elegant Miss Sinclair enjoy the company of Mr. Miles Crane?

"Oh, of course," Miles was answering in his deep voice. "Lizbeth will be delighted to see you. And thank you again, by the way, for the cranberry bread and the pillow you so thoughtfully brought my aunt."

"Oh, it was nothing." Caroline flushed with genuine pleasure.

"Caroline is an absolute wonder," Miles explained to Lara. "Here she is, a busy attorney, yet she still manages to find the time to bake bread and hand-stitch a patchwork pillow for Aunt Lizbeth."

"How nice!" Lara nodded approvingly. *I hate her*, she grumbled to herself. Home-baked bread! Patchwork pillows! Busy, glamorous female lawyer on the go! What else did this superwoman do? Lara wondered.

"Which reminds me," Caroline said, placing a slender hand on Miles's bare arm. "You must take a look at the new Cessna I've been considering. I'd like your opinion about the lease option."

"Really, Caroline," Miles protested with a chuckle. "My advice would be meaningless. You know ten times more about flying than I do."

I definitely hate her. Lara sighed inwardly. Oh, good heavens! Was this possible? Was this sudden outpouring of hostility caused by what she thought it was? Jealousy? Is this what it feels like? Lara marveled. Less than a week ago, she couldn't have cared at all whether or not Miles Crane eloped to Mars with ten Las Vegas showgirls. Now, inexplicably, a black fury was starting to bubble inside of her. Lara was seized with the strangest desire to accidentally drop a slice of Yankee Town Fair blueberry pie right down the front of Miss Caroline Sinclair's immaculate white linen suit. Oh, this was disastrous! Lara groaned. How in the world had it happened? She was actually experiencing the emotion of jealousy and the object of this mad inner turmoil was none other than Miles Crane! Terrific. Wonderful. Swell. Was it any coincidence that Lara wrote comedy for a living? The absolute absurdity of the situation was staggering.

"Well, I'll see you on Monday, Miles," Caroline was saying with a slightly plaintive note in her voice. "Maybe we can have lunch."

"That's a good idea." Miles nodded. "I'd like to go over that deposition."

"Nice meeting you." Caroline glanced at Lara briefly.

"Same here." Lara smiled thinly, and wondered why she had never bothered to learn how to bake, sew or even fly a single-engine aircraft.

"Sweet kid," Miles observed as Caroline walked off toward the other end of the park. "It's her first year in practice and I've sort of taken her under my wing."

"I'll just *bet* you have!"

Miles quirked an eyebrow. "Excuse me, Lara?"

Lara was taken aback by the acidness in her own tone, but couldn't stop herself from adding sarcastically, "She seems so frail and helpless, too!"

"Oh, not Caroline," Miles went on, oblivious to the tight line of Lara's lips. "For someone who is only twenty-six years old, she's a regular go-getter! I think the two of you could be great friends."

"I'm *sure*."

Miles looked at Lara, completely mystified. What had come over her, all of a sudden? Just a few minutes ago, she seemed so happy and cheerful, as if she was actually having a good time in his company. But now—Miles was unsure. Perhaps he had overrated his own ability to keep someone as bright and vivacious as Lara entertained. Maybe he was just as dull and boring as he had ever been. He regarded her out of the corner of his eye. Lord, she was so beautiful today, in that sexy pink dress. More beautiful than all his past memories. The gold locket glinted in the bright July sun, and Miles recalled how his fingers had nearly trembled when he'd fastened the delicate chain around Lara's neck. Her skin had felt like silk where his hands had briefly touched it. All he could think of was how much he longed to touch Lara again. But this time, a lingering touch. The way he had come so close that afternoon on the beach at Minawin Island. Who knows what might have happened if those idiot teenagers hadn't blundered so rudely onto the scene? Perhaps he had frightened her, back there, Miles thought uncomfortably. Or even worse, maybe he'd just made a silly jerk out of himself. For an instant, he'd actually succeeded in convincing himself that Lara might have welcomed his kiss. At least he'd managed to spare himself the embarrassment of her rejection, Miles decided. He cleared his throat.

"Would you care for something to drink, Lara?" Well, he had so say *something*.

"That would be nice," she replied. She was somewhat annoyed with herself, if the truth be told. Normally her natural disposition was cheerful and sunny. "Mellow" was what her friends and colleagues called her, and to a Californian, that was the ultimate accolade. Now, she was overwhelmed by irritability.

"How about some fresh lemonade?" Miles pointed in the direction of the yellow-and-white striped refreshment tent.

"Lemonade sounds great," she replied with a sigh. Oh, maybe this sudden irritability had nothing at all to do with Miles or that insufferably perfect Miss Caroline Sinclair, or anyone else for that matter. Maybe it was jet lag, pure and simple, and the sooner she was safely back in Los Angeles, the better.

A few minutes later, the two of them were strolling across the green with tall, plastic glasses of fresh-squeezed lemonade, courtesy of the Pine Harbor Women's Auxiliary.

"Lara," Miles started hesitantly, "why don't we sit down for a minute?" He guided her to one of the beautiful, old oak trees that had stood majestically overlooking the harbor for more than a century.

Lara lowered herself gingerly to the grass and tucked her legs underneath her skirt. Miles eased down next to her. For a long moment, neither of them said a word. Finally, Miles said with a weary note in his voice, "I'm sorry, Lara."

She looked at him in surprise. "Sorry? For what?" *For liking that bimbo, Caroline?*

"For dragging you along to the fair. I realize that after your Hollywood parties and glamorous celebrities, this all must seem pretty boring."

It was Lara's turn to be nonplussed. "I *beg* your pardon?"

"Oh, don't try to hide it, Lara." Miles shook his head insistently. "And don't try to be polite, either. I can tell you're not having a very good time."

"What on earth are you talking about, Miles?"

"I realize you went along with this to please Aunt Lizbeth, but it isn't necessary to drag the day out any more than we have to." He paused. "Besides, I get the impression that the last thing you need after six years away from Pine Harbor is to have old memories stirred up by the Yankee Town Fair."

There was a strange sadness in his silver eyes. Was it almost a look of defeat? Lara could not be sure.

"You're wrong, Miles," Lara responded quietly.

"Am I?" His expression was taut.

"You know nothing about the way I feel."

"On the contrary, I think I know quite well." There was an inexplicable flicker of sadness across his gaunt face. "This town is filled with unhappy memories for you, Lara. That's why you left here six years ago and haven't been back since." He paused. "Don't you think I'm aware of it? Every July, you and Jason used to wreak your own particular brand of mischief at the fair. I remember the year you put a tiny guppy in each glass of lemonade." He glanced at his drink with distaste. Actually, it had been rather humorous, Miles recalled. "I remember other things, too." There was a long silence. He was remembering that it was at the Yankee Town Fair, when Lara was seventeen, that Jason had proposed to her. That bittersweet memory had to be the reason for Lara's sudden change of mood, Miles thought glumly. Of course, that was it! What else could it possibly be?

"You're wrong," Lara repeated quietly. "You have no way of knowing what goes on in my mind, Miles Crane."

"Oh, I've got a pretty good idea," came the pained reply.

"If you must know—" Lara eyed him steadily "—I was just thinking of a particularly happy memory, at this precise moment." She hadn't been thinking about Jason at all, as a matter of fact. How curious! "I was remembering my tenth birthday."

Miles quirked an eyebrow in astonishment. It was the last thing he had expected Lara to remember. "Your tenth birthday..." he repeated more to himself than aloud.

Lara nodded. "I was sitting here alone, under this very tree, wearing that scratchy, frilly pink party dress that Aunt Lizbeth had bought me in Boston."

"I remember." Miles gave a faint smile.

He'd just come home from college and blundered into a house filled with a mob of boisterous nine- and ten-year-olds in party hats throwing ice cream, cake and water balloons at each other. Well, it wasn't as if Lara MacEuan's birthday parties had ever been quiet, subdued affairs, he remembered thinking, and then had realized that the little girl was nowhere to be found. It wasn't till half an hour later that Miles spotted her up on the hill, sitting under the oak tree, tear stains on her young face. When he'd asked her why she was crying, Lara had blurted out that her parents had promised to be there for her birthday *this* time. Of course, Miles recalled cynically, Willy and Denise had never come. They had been off somewhere on another exotic adventure.

Lara gazed at Miles. "I remember you took a linen handkerchief out of your pocket, and wiped my eyes. You told me that sometimes grown-ups were just like children."

Strange, Lara thought now. In all the ensuing years, she had somehow forgotten how Miles had leaned back against this same tree and started to tell her stories of magical ships and enchanted islands on the far side of the world. It had made Lara stop crying and imagine that her young parents were adventurers in a fairy tale conjured up by the lure of the sea. Afterward Miles had reached into his pocket again, this time pulling out a Chinese puzzle ring. "A special, magic ring for your birthday, little princess," he had said with a faint smile.

Strange, the memory of that day had eluded Lara until now. Perhaps it was because she and Miles had never been that close again since. It had been a moment of friendship the two of them somehow had never shared afterward. An enchanted afternoon that had faded as quickly as it had come to life. How odd, to suddenly recall that forgotten memory after nearly fifteen years.

"Thank you for what you did that day, Miles," Lara said.

"I didn't think you remembered." He gazed off into the distant water.

"Maybe I didn't . . . until now." She paused. "You were very kind and patient." He'd also kissed her on the cheek, she thought.

At that moment, Miles seemed to read her mind. "Yes, I did kiss you, didn't I?"

"Yes, you did." Lara felt the oddest sensation in the pit of her stomach. She wasn't ten years old anymore and a kiss from Miles Crane now meant something totally different.

Something strange seemed to light in his silver-blue eyes. "I kissed your cheek, Lara."

"Yes."

Miles slowly turned his head toward Lara. "Was it like this?" His voice was practically a rasp as he reached out and took Lara's face in his hands. Tentatively, his lips brushed one cheek, then the other.

Lara's senses tingled. "I . . . I don't think it was like that, Miles." Her words came out breathless.

"No, I don't suppose it was," he murmured with an odd tremor in his own voice. "And it probably wasn't like this, either." Miles lowered his hard mouth to Lara's lips and gave her a brief, shattering kiss.

Chapter Five

Nothing was the same afterward. It was more than Miles's kiss. It was also the revived memory of a magic moment the two of them had shared on a summer's day so many years past. Of course, the first time Miles kissed Lara on the lips was more than just shattering in a physical sense. It was an emotional jolt that served to open her eyes wider than they ever had been before. From that moment on, whenever Lara heard the name Jason Crane, her response would surely be: "Jason *who*?" He suddenly no longer existed. The name Miles now had a magic all its own.

But Lara was well aware that she might have gone from the frying pan directly into the fire. She had been badly hurt once before and she had no intention of being hurt again. She found Miles devastatingly attractive, but the fact remained that the man was still an enigma. It was possible for a person to kiss someone and have it mean nothing but a momentary impulse. For all Lara knew, Miles might be seriously involved with Caroline Sinclair. Or any number of other women, for that matter. It was possible he carried some secret torch for an unnamed female. There was absolutely no way Lara could tell for sure. She had been in Pine Harbor only a few days. It was sort of like coming into the movie theater in the middle of a film.

In any event, Lara thought, the subject was actually moot. In a week she would be on her way back to Los Angeles and probably never see Miles Crane again.

"Did you two have a nice time today?" Lizbeth asked when they visited her late in the afternoon.

"Very nice." Miles looked at Lara.

"Yes, very pleasant." Lara smiled brightly. For some reason she didn't want Miles to see how much his brief kiss had affected her.

Miles sensed Lara's discomfort, but was unsure of the cause. He cleared his throat. "Aunt, by the way, we ran into Caroline."

"Who?"

"Oh, for heaven's sake, Aunt. Caroline Sinclair, from the office. Remember that cranberry bread she baked you last week. And the pillow?"

Lizbeth seemed distracted. "Oh, Caroline, yes. Nice girl, but a little too tall."

Lara's lips twitched, and this slight gesture was not unnoticed by Lizbeth. "Do me a favor, dear." The elderly woman shook her head. "Don't ever bake me cranberry bread."

Lara grinned. "You can count on that, Auntie."

Miles seemed bewildered. "But I thought you loved cranberry bread. You told Caroline it was your favorite."

Lizbeth rolled her eyes. "Miles, couldn't you tell that I was merely being polite to the young lady? I certainly didn't want to hurt her feelings, dear."

"Oh, well." Miles was completely confounded.

"And don't make me any pillows, either," Lizbeth said to her goddaughter. "I have enough pillows, for goodness' sake!"

"No worries there!" Lara nodded cheerfully.

"I don't understand any of this." Miles was completely lost at sea.

"What don't you understand, Miles?" Lizbeth scoffed. "That some young hussy is chasing you with a pitchfork?"

"What are you talking about?"

"Blind as a bat." Lizbeth shook her head. "A typical man!" She glanced over at Lara. "I assume that *you* understand, don't you, dear?"

Lara found herself staring at Miles head-on. "Oh, I certainly understand."

"Understand *what*?" Miles stared back, totally exasperated.

"She's not exactly chasing him with a pitchfork, Auntie." Lara eyed Miles steadily. "I think it's more like a Cessna."

"A what?" asked Lizbeth.

"Are you talking about Caroline?" The meaning of the conversation finally dawned on Miles.

"Bingo!" Lara smiled blandly.

"You're kidding, aren't you?" Miles's expression grew odd.

"We know what we're talking about. Pillows! Breads! That girl is chasing you!"

"Of all the—" Miles shook his head in disbelief.

"Yes, the hussy is definitely chasing him, Lara," Lizbeth repeated.

Lara shrugged. "I think she already may have caught him, Auntie."

"Is that what you think, Lara?" Miles ignored his aunt completely, the strangest glimmer in his silvery eyes. "Is that what you really think after what happened today?"

"I don't know what to think." Lara lowered her eyes to the ground. She really *didn't* know, to be totally truthful.

"Wait a minute!" Lizbeth piped up. "What happened today? What are you two talking about?"

"Nothing much, Aunt." Miles continued to stare at Lara.

"Oh, nothing much!" Lara raised her head in annoyance. "Is that what you call that kiss? Nothing much?"

"A kiss?" exclaimed Lizbeth. "*What* kiss?"

"The kiss I gave Lara this afternoon." Miles's voice sounded strange.

"*You* kissed Lara?"

"Just a little kiss, Auntie." Lara shrugged. "I'm sure it isn't any different than the ones he gives to all the other girls."

"All the other girls?" Miles boomed. "What other girls are you talking about?"

"Of course, you have lots of other girls mooning around you besides Caroline," Lara went on carelessly.

"What do you think?" Miles's jaw practically dropped. "That I actually have some kind of harem? Then you really must be one heck of a comedy writer!"

"You kissed Lara?" Lizbeth repeated slowly, staring at her great-nephew.

"Believe me, Miles Crane," Lara scoffed, "if this were one of my *Hap Harrigan* scripts, Caroline Sinclair would have slipped on a banana peel and disappeared down an open manhole in Scene One!"

"Oh, is that so?" Miles's eyes grew bright, the dawning comprehension in his face. "Are you trying to tell me something, Lara?"

"Not at all!" she denied hotly.

"Well, then," Lizbeth was reasoning it all out, "if the two of you kissed each other—"

"We didn't kiss each other, Auntie," Lara insisted. "*He* kissed me. I most certainly did not kiss *him*!"

"That's not the way *I* remember it." Miles folded his arms against his chest.

"But this is just wonderful news." Lizbeth ignored both of them. "A romantic kiss at the fair! Of course, I realize exactly what this means, darlings."

"What does it mean, Aunt?" Miles asked dryly.

"Why, that my two favorite young people are, how do they say it these days? 'Going together'!"

Lara was mortified. "Oh, Auntie!"

"Why, I'm just so thrilled I can't stand it!" Lizbeth was gushing. "In my wildest dreams, I never imagined—" The elderly woman sat up straight. "Why, I feel twenty years younger already! To think that just a few minutes ago, I thought I was going to have another relapse, but now, oh! Children, you've made me the happiest old woman in the world!"

Miles stood there silently, listening to his great aunt's excited rambling. He took a deep breath. "I'm glad you feel that way, Aunt." Slowly he turned to Lara. "Because, more than anything else, Lara and I both love you and want your happiness." He paused significantly. "*Don't* we, Lara?"

"Of... of course, we do." What was all this about, anyhow, Lara wondered.

Miles took several long strides over to Lara, and casually placed an arm around her waist. "Yes, you're quite correct, Aunt. Lara and I are, as you say, going together." He shot Lara a sharp glance. "*Aren't* we?"

Lara swallowed nervously. "I don't... I mean, it isn't exactly—" she stammered.

Lizbeth seemed concerned. "Lara, dear. Are you saying it isn't so? That Miles is mistaken?" Her face went almost ashen. "Did the two of you have some silly quarrel?" She almost trembled. "I can't bear to think such a thing!"

"Oh, it was just a little argument," Miles interjected smoothly. "It's all cleared up now, isn't it, Lara?" His stare was intense.

Just play along with this, his expression was telegraphing loud and clear to Lara. *Can't you see how badly she needs to believe it?* his eyes begged.

"Yes." Lara nodded slowly. "It's all cleared up now." She hesitated. "Just a silly little argument."

"Well, then," Lizbeth declared resolutely, "shouldn't the two of you kiss and make up?"

Miles's silver eyes had an odd glint. "As a matter of fact, we should." He paused significantly. "*Shouldn't* we, Lara?"

She gave a nervous swallow. "I...that is, well, yes, we should, I suppose."

"Absolutely," Lizbeth asserted.

"Absolutely," Miles echoed. "Come here, sweetheart!" Before Lara had a chance to protest, he had pulled her into his arms and lowered his mouth to hers. There was a startling electricity to Miles's kiss. "Lara," he suddenly whispered against her ear, "for appearances' sake, I really think you ought to put your arms around me, at least."

Blindly, Lara complied with his urgent request, reaching up on her tiptoes and wrapping her arms around his neck. Somehow, as if it was the most natural action in the world, she found herself pressing up against his hard frame, her slender fingers unconsciously exploring the short, silky thickness of his blond hair. Was it her imagination or did Miles actually tremble?

"Lara," he whispered in amazement.

"What?" she asked with a soft sigh against the tense cord of his throat, and Miles gave an involuntary shudder, pulling abruptly out of the embrace.

"We've made up, Aunt." He managed to find his voice. Lord, Miles was thinking. He'd come perilously close to losing all pretense of control. If he hadn't put some distance between himself and Lara a moment ago, he wouldn't have been answerable for his actions.

"Yes." Lara felt a flush suffuse her cheeks. "We've settled our differences, Auntie."

Had she just been playacting now? Miles wondered. When he'd asked her to go along with the charade for Aunt Lizbeth's benefit, Miles had naturally expected Lara to cooperate just a little. He hadn't asked for heaven. Her enthusiastic response had very nearly pushed him over the edge. That teasingly brief kiss under the old oak tree had been child's play compared to what had just transpired. "Yes, we certainly have." He gave a perfunctory nod that belied the tumult raging inside of him. "As a lawyer, I can attest to the fact that no differences are truly irreconcilable." He groaned inwardly. What a stupid, inane

thing to say! Had he really just made such a preten-
tious remark?

"Children, I'm just so pleased!" Lizbeth was chattering on. "You make such a lovely couple." She
paused curiously. "*So*, Miles?"

He quirked an eyebrow. "Yes, Aunt?"

"It's Saturday night." She looked at him questioningly. "What are your plans, dear?"

"Plans?" Miles asked vaguely.

"Isn't Saturday the most important night of the
week for young couples? So, where are you taking
Lara on your date tonight?"

"Our...date?" Lara repeated shakily.

"Let me guess!" the elderly woman cried out en-
thusiastically. "You're going out dancing! How absolutely divine! A marvelous idea!"

"Dancing, hmm," Miles murmured. "What do you
think, Lara?"

"I...well, that is." She was suddenly self-conscious.
"I'm a bit out of practice."

"That makes two of us," Miles replied smoothly. In
truth, it went beyond simply being out of practice. He
happened to be the world's worst dancer. On the other
hand, when would he have a better excuse to hold Lara
closely against him? Only an idiot would let such a
golden opportunity pass him by. "Yes, Aunt," Miles
said, nodding matter-of-factly. "As it happens, I *am*
taking Lara out dancing. How on earth did you ever
guess?"

Chapter Six

Just a few days and several thousand miles ago in Los Angeles, had anyone informed Lara that she'd be spending a Saturday night out dining and dancing with Miles Crane, it might have sounded like the biggest joke in the world. Nothing, it seemed, was turning out the way Lara had originally expected.

In the first place, she had half-expected to find her beloved godmother Lizbeth practically on her deathbed. Never had Lara considered the possibility of the old woman's sudden and near-miraculous recovery. In the second place, she had braced herself in fearful expectation of unpleasant memories from the past, and those unpleasant memories had never quite materialized. In the third place, Lara still expected to feel depressed about the plum summer writing assignment that she had been forced to lose. Instead, she felt curiously unperturbed about the disappointing setback in her television career. At the moment all that concerned her were the people and events here in Pine Harbor.

Miles had mentioned plans for dinner at the nearby town of Eastport, and then named several clubs they might visit afterward. A genuine, textbook date. Lara twisted her lips pensively. When was the last time she'd gone out on one of those? She glanced at the clock on her bureau. Eight o'clock was the time they had agreed upon, and that gave Lara less than half an hour to get ready. She rifled through the contents of the closet and realized that nothing was as simple or more suitable than the skirt and silk blouse that still lay neatly packed away in her canvas carryall. The last thing she felt like wearing was an outfit replete with frills and bows. Somehow it might communicate the wrong idea to Miles.

What wrong idea? she asked herself in front of the mirror a few minutes later, studying the sleek line of the tailored navy skirt and neatly tucked-in ivory blouse. Did it have anything at all to do with the fact that she still hadn't figured out Miles's real motivation for this evening's date? Well, yes, as it so happened. After the little charade in Lizbeth's room, Lara had been left in a state of utter turmoil and confusion. It was bad enough that Miles's passionate embrace had left her practically breathless. Worse still, she remained unsure about Miles's intentions. Lara

was convinced that he had actually trembled during
their embrace, but what if it had all been a perfectly
engineered performance for the sole benefit of Great-
Aunt Lizbeth? Her experience with men had been so
limited, Lara had no idea what to think. How much of
this "date" was genuine? Perhaps she was taking this
all too seriously. Maybe women reacted in such a way
when they hadn't been kissed in years and years. Every
gesture and vital, masculine embrace acquired a sig-
nificance that was completely unwarranted.

Besides, Lara grimaced at the mirror, today she had
witnessed a whole new side to Miles. Relaxed, confident and popular. Scores of people had greeted him at
the Yankee Town Fair this afternoon with a mixture
of admiration and respect. During the brief exchange
with Chubby Winslow, it had not escaped Lara's de-
tection that the most popular fellow in her high school
graduating class had struck up a comfortable rapport
with Miles. The latter had ambled through the fair
with an ease and confidence Lara had never credited
him with. In the past few years, Miles Crane had es-
tablished himself as a leading figure in the business
and social fabric of Pine Harbor. *Social fabric.* Now
that was an interesting expression. She rolled her eyes.
Hadn't Lara read stories of shy, introverted boys who
had matured into self-assured men of the world? It
was growing apparent that Miles was that kind of
man. For all she knew, the successful attorney had
half a dozen women on a string. After all, he *was* a
Crane. And if Caroline Sinclair was any indication,

the man's nightly datebook must be filled. Lara gave a weary sigh. Somehow, she felt far less uneasiness with Miles when she still believed him to be shy and plodding. Lara was distinctly uncomfortable when she thought of the word that now perfectly described this evening's date with Miles: *unpredictable.*

It had become almost a ritual. For the second time in one day, Miles and Lara presented themselves to Lizbeth before going out on their date. The elderly woman gave a nod of approval at their appearance. Miles had changed into beige slacks and a sports jacket. He looked almost collegiate, Lara thought with a half-smile. In fact, he looked ten years younger. He might have been on his way to a fraternity party.

"I've never seen that coat before." Lizbeth pursed her lips.

"It's new, Aunt," Miles explained, unable to take his eyes away from Lara. In that short, pencil-slim skirt and gently clinging silk blouse, she looked so sexy he seriously wondered how he was going to survive this evening. He ran a serious risk of making a first-class fool out of himself tonight, that was for sure. Miles stared appreciatively at the slender line of Lara's legs.

"And Lara, dear," Lizbeth was saying. "You look very lovely in that outfit. Doesn't she, Miles?"

"Yes, lovely," Miles agreed huskily. Wild, exciting possibilities paraded themselves tauntingly through his imagination. Fate had played into his hands so far, and had bestowed upon him this unexpected chance with Lara. Bless Great-Aunt Lizbeth for giving him this incredible opportunity with Lara MacEuan. Miles felt like a nervous schoolboy beneath the cool facade. He prayed for Lara to want him, just a little. Otherwise he was going to make an idiot of himself tonight.

"So, where are you taking Lara for dinner?" Lizbeth quizzed her nephew.

Miles dragged his silver eyes away from Lara. "I thought we'd go to Ryan's Mill Inn."

"Excellent choice," Lizbeth said nodding approvingly. "Don't you agree, Lara?"

"Yes, Auntie." *Ryan's Mill*! Probably the most exclusive, expensive restaurant in the entire county. And with its own waterfall and stream gliding past the terraces of the inn, it was also considered to be by far the most romantic. Lara shuddered deliciously at the implication, and then remembered the real motivation behind the glamorous date. This was all being done to impress Aunt Lizbeth. Had she forgotten *that* so quickly. Lara couldn't help but notice the way the old woman's blue eyes positively lit up when Miles mentioned their elegant destination for the evening. Lara chided herself. It would serve her well to be reminded that this wasn't even a real date. She and Miles were merely playing roles in a performance strictly for the benefit of the ailing Lizbeth Crane.

Lara glanced over at her tall, lanky companion. His gaunt features revealed nothing to her, his expression was aggravatingly bland. Cool, calm and collected,

Lara thought with a thin smile. For all she could tell, Miles would rather be spending the evening with the pretty, multitalented Caroline Sinclair. Perhaps the couple spent every Saturday dancing the night away. Who really knew anything about Miles Crane and his personal life? The man was turning out to be a complete and utter mystery. Lara's talents and perceptions lay strictly in the area of comedy. Slapstick humor was so simple and direct. It was totally open and aboveboard, hiding nothing from the audience. It was honest and all-revealing, unlike the murky convolutions of the suspense genre. And if there was anything Lara didn't care for one bit, it was a mystery.

The drive to the restaurant in Miles's Mercedes was uneventful. For the most part, Miles kept his eyes on the winding country road and exchanged occasional pleasantries with Lara. It was as if the passionate embrace a few hours before had never even occurred. For some odd reason, this was both a source of relief and mild irritation to Lara.

"Things haven't changed much, have they?" Miles remarked conversationally.

"What?" Lara was startled. Did he mean between them?

Miles glanced at her curiously. "Don't you agree that they haven't really changed?" He paused. "No new buildings have gone up on this road in the past few years. It's stayed relatively unspoiled and free from development. Don't you prefer things this way, Lara?''

"Of, of course. Certainly. Who wouldn't?'' Lara tried to quiet the butterflies in her stomach. What had she thought Miles had been talking about? Obviously the last thing in the world the man wanted to discuss was the nonexistent relationship between the two of them.

Miles quirked a curious eyebrow. He found himself unable to gage Lara's hesitant response. Damn, he thought with annoyance. She must be remembering how often she and Jason rode their bicycles down this rural highway. Something, anything at all, that had to do with the distant past. Lara's mind certainly wasn't on the present, and it wasn't on *him*, that was for sure. Miles gripped the leather-covered steering wheel with tense fingers. Somehow, someway, he was going to do his best to make Lara forget Jason had ever existed. The only man he wanted her to think about was himself. Abruptly he cleared his throat. "Yes, I was just observing how little things seem to change in the country." Miles forced a bright, conversational tone to his voice. It was a brightness he wasn't feeling at all. "I bet it isn't this lush and green out in Los Angeles." Well, that was pretty inane, Miles thought deprecatingly, but at least it was better than nothing.

"No, it isn't this green." Lara didn't want to talk about the weather, the leaves or obscure little country roads. She wanted Miles to look into her eyes and tell her how attractively she was dressed this evening, and that super Amazon women like Caroline Sinclair did nothing for him. *That's* what Lara wanted Miles to talk about. She gave an inner sigh of secret exasperation.

"I mean," Miles murmured, staring at the road ahead, "there must be some greener parts of Los Angeles, such as the landscaped and elegantly manicured estates of Bel Air, but you don't have the rolling meadows and wooded knolls that we have right here in New England." Oh, good grief! Miles wanted to bite off his tongue. Had he really just rambled on like a moronic travel video? So far, his golden opportunity with Lara was failing miserably. This conversation was going about as well as a shuffleboard match aboard the *Titanic*.

"Yes, New England is greener," Lara replied tonelessly. Well, this was certainly exciting. Miles seemed to be about as interested in her as he would be in a toothache. It was bad enough that Lara's considerable skill at clever conversation had completely deserted her. She had never been this tongue-tied, even back in the early throes of her girlhood crush on Jason. What had happened to all the lilting and sharp flashes of wit that she was paid so handsomely to help create for Hap Harrigan each week?

At last they arrived at the restaurant. Ryan's Mill Inn was a historic building constructed of wood and stone, and boasted the most picturesque setting in all of Connecticut. It was situated directly on the river, with one dining area actually perched below a waterfall. Inside, the fully restored building was a cool and serene rustic haven with rich, wood floors and ceiling-high windows, which afforded stunning water views in all directions.

After a valet had taken the car, Miles led Lara into the anteroom, where a smiling hostess in a floor-length calico gown escorted them to their table.

"Would you care for a drink?" Miles asked with almost studied politeness after the two of them had been seated by an open window.

"Yes, please," she replied, nodding quickly. Although Lara seldom drank as a rule, a glass of white wine just now might work wonders. Meanwhile she tried to distract herself by gazing at a family of ducks as they paddled unperturbed in a single line along the river.

Miles placed the order with their waiter, and after a few minutes of vague, polite conversation, the drinks arrived. He lifted up his glass of scotch and held it out toward Lara. "A toast to Aunt Lizbeth," he declared quietly. "May she grow healthier and happier with every passing day."

"I'll second that." Lara's wineglass clinked against his own. "A worthy sentiment," she said sincerely. At last, Lara thought, a topic that held meaning for both of them.

"You do realize—" Miles set his glass down and regarded her for a long moment "—that the incredible improvement in Lizbeth's condition is due completely to you, Lara."

"Oh, I wouldn't say that, Miles." She took another sip of the California Chablis. It felt so warm and glowing.

"*I* would."

"Lizbeth's unexpected turn for the better is simply the result of a combination of factors," Lara protested.

Miles stared at her intently. "What's the matter, Lara? Since when were you unable to accept a compliment?"

"It has nothing to do—"

"Oh, yes," he finished for her. "It has everything to do with you."

Lara took several more sips of the wine. Already the room had begun to grow rather warm. "You're assuming that her physical condition could be affected completely by emotions. That's not very realistic." Why was she arguing with him? Lara wondered.

"And since when have you gotten so modest? I suppose you have always been well aware, Lara, that you could wrap my great-aunt around your little finger since the day you were born."

She pressed her lips together. "Oh, don't exaggerate."

"Who's exaggerating?" Miles leaned forward across the table. "It's a simple fact. You happen to be one of those rare people who possess this, well, magic."

Lara practically spilled her wine. Was she imagining it, or had Miles just given her a unique compliment? "What kind of magic?" She tried to sound casual.

He gazed at her for a long moment. "You know very well what I'm talking about."

"No, I don't." Lara shook her head firmly.

"Oh, I believe you do." Miles reached out his hand and touched Lara's gently. "You must have always been aware of that special magnetism you possess."

Magnetism? Was this man actually sitting across the table and telling her she had *magnetism*? Miles Crane, who had given her about as many compliments during her lifetime as Lara had fingers on one hand? Miles Crane thought she possessed some magical quality? "No, I'm not aware of it." Lara tried to sound blasé.

"And by the way, Lara." Miles's hand suddenly tightened on hers. "My aunt isn't the only person you've always been able to wrap around your finger." Miles hadn't meant to say that. The words had just sort of blurted out. Oh, blame the scotch and soda.

Lara felt an odd quiver. "Who else are you talking about, Miles?"

"Who else, indeed." There was a long pause.

Lara stared back at him in utter astonishment, trying to fathom the expression in his gray eyes. She cleared her throat uncomfortably. "Honestly, Miles. How would I know what you mean? I'm not exactly a mind reader, in case you hadn't noticed."

He smiled cryptically. "Oh, I noticed. I definitely noticed *that*, Lara." Before he could say another word, the waiter arrived to take their dinner order.

Dinner was a pleasant affair. They both shared a Caesar salad, which was followed by a rack of lamb for Miles and the poached Norwegian salmon with capers for Lara. Curiously enough, whatever it was that Miles had been about to say before being interrupted by the waiter, he obviously preferred to keep to himself. But the conversation developed an easy flow of its own, with no more awkward pauses. Perhaps, Lara thought, it had to do with the bottle of wine that Miles had ordered to go along with the dinner. Whatever the cause, both of them were considerably more relaxed and at ease than they had been at the beginning of the evening. Maybe it would turn out to be a delightful date after all.

By the time they reached the dessert course, Miles had become quite the charming host. He asked Lara to tell him more about her life in Los Angeles and seemed truly interested in her answers.

"So, the weekly television series grind isn't as glamorous as most people think it is?" Miles asked, setting down his coffee cup and reaching for a cigarette.

"It's not glamorous at all," Lara said, shaking her head.

"Don't tell me you're actually bored with it?"

"Not bored exactly." She sighed. "It's just that I feel there are other things that are more important, somehow."

"Such as?"

She looked across the table. "I don't know. Friends. Family." The truth was, she had never gotten over the feeling of being alone in a sea of strangers ever since moving to California.

Miles's eyes narrowed. "Lara." His voice sounded odd. "You know you'll always have a family right here in Pine Harbor."

"I know that," she murmured automatically.

"Do you? Do you really?" Miles prodded firmly. "Do you truly understand how very much a part of our lives you've always been?"

Our lives? Lara thought. *Our* lives? What on earth was Miles trying to say to her? She swallowed and took the plunge. "I never thought I was much a part of *your* life, Miles." Well, it was the truth, wasn't it? For the most part, Miles had spent his younger years ignoring both Lara and Jason. He'd almost made a point of ignoring them, in fact.

"You were always a part of my life," Miles said quietly. "It's just that you were probably too busy to notice."

If a hand grenade had been thrown into the dining room at that moment, Lara would not have been aware of it. There was a long pause, and the butterflies began fluttering inside her stomach again. "What are you trying to say to me, Miles?" she uttered softly.

"Haven't you been listening, Lara?" Miles drew a deep breath. "You've always been something special to me." There. It was out. He'd finally said it. Miles was strangely relieved.

Perhaps it was the wine, but Lara suddenly felt light-headed. "Well, that's nice to know."

"Nice?" He glanced at her. "You think it's *nice*?"

Lara shook her head and leaned forward, resting her chin on her hands. "Let me clarify that, Miles Crane. I think it's *very* nice." Did she sound calm? Inside, Lara's heart was racing. Just how *special* did Miles mean, anyhow? After all, there was "special," and then there was *special*.

"Very nice?" came Miles's low response. "Do you mean that, Lara?" He reached across the table and grasped her wrist. "Does that mean you're pleased?"

Pleased? Lara thought. Now, there was another interesting word. "Yes, Miles." The wine had given her more courage. "Hasn't it occurred to you by now that I would be very pleased to know that you like me?"

"Like?" Miles looked at her strangely. "Oh, honey, I'd say it's far beyond *like*."

Honey? Lara gave a convulsive swallow. It was the very first endearment she could remember Miles giving her. And what else had he just said? About his feelings going far beyond just liking. What on earth did he mean by that? Was Lara being terribly dense? "What do you mean?" She tried to sound casual.

"Oh, I think you know just what I mean, Lara." Miles ran a tanned finger up the bare skin of her forearm, and Lara tingled. There was another long silence and then he pulled his hand away abruptly. Was he out of his mind, Miles chastened himself, going on like some kind of lovesick schoolboy? In another minute, he might have started confessing all sorts of things that were far too personal to risk saying right now. The last thing Miles wanted to do was make a total idiot out of himself. And he had just come perilously close to winning the Dunce of the Year award. He cleared his throat sharply. "Are you ready to go dancing?"

She looked at him in absolute bewilderment. What was the explanation for this sudden change of mood? "Uh, sure, Miles," Lara agreed quickly. "I'm ready."

It was a small, out-of-the-way roadhouse. The kind one often sees scattered throughout America, just off one country highway or another. This one was called Vinnie's Blue Grotto, and since Lara could remember, the long, single-story structure had been a favorite nightspot in the county, especially with the over-thirty crowd. The owner had once played with some of the big bands of the forties and fifties. Now, he enjoyed running his tiny club with nostalgic live music on the weekends, and highly forgettable cuisine the rest of the week. When Lara and Miles entered the establishment, it was already packed with couples. As always, the lighting was rather dim. It lent the club a romantic ambiance.

It seemed like the most natural thing in the world when Miles finally held out his hand and led Lara onto the crowded dance floor. She found herself tightly pressed up against Miles's corduroy sports jacket. Every step the two of them took, it seemed that the crush of couples around them continued to push them closer and closer together. It was an indescribable sensation to be held so close against Miles's hard frame.

"I'm not the world's best dancer," he confessed softly against Lara's ear as they moved slowly to the strains of Duke Ellington's classic "Satin Doll."

"Neither am I," Lara murmured against his chest. It was seductively delicious to feel the warmth of his chest through the thin cotton of his button-down shirt.

"You dance just fine, Lara," Miles breathed against her hair. "Believe me." It was criminal, he mused to himself, just how much he was enjoying this moment. Lara's hair smelled of the light, floral after-bath splash she always used, and it was sheer delight to be able to hold her this close. Lara didn't even seem aware of Miles's lips brushing soft, stolen kisses across her hair. What had ever made him care that he didn't know how to dance? What did it matter than he had two left feet? Miles realized that it simply did not matter. Dancing was all a state of mind, he thought as his firm hands spread possessively over the fine silken material covering Lara's straight back.

Lara was barely able to stifle a gasp as Miles drew her even closer, every curve of her body making electric contact with his own. She could feel the hard lines of his muscular thighs and the beat of his heart through the oxford shirt.

"You're adorable," Miles said as his lips brushed the delicate skin of her earlobe. "Did you know that, Lara?" At this very moment he could not imagine being any closer to heaven.

She barely heard his words, but their effect was to make her feel light-headed. Of course, to be completely logical, it might very well have been just the wine from dinner that made her feel this way. She was conscious of the spicy cologne that Miles had worn as long as she could remember. It was so distinctly *him*. How could she have previously thought it to be an ordinary, unexceptional scent? Now, it only served to heighten Lara's awareness and inflame her senses. She allowed herself the luxury of relaxing against him at long last.

"Lara!" Miles exclaimed in surprise, and stared down at her with glittering silver eyes.

"What?" She gazed up into those wonderful eyes and was lost. Without speaking she asked a question she had been unable to put into words, her own eyes and lips an open invitation.

"God," he uttered softly. "What are you doing to me?" Miles's loose-fitting jacket and slacks could not conceal the hardness of his muscles.

"Miles," she breathed in astonishment. The proximity of his frank maleness was almost a shock to her.

"The way you say my name!" he marveled with a shake of his head. "Say it again, honey."

The endearment gave Lara a secret, inner smile. "Miles," she repeated tentatively.

"Yes," came the husky nod of approval. "That's the way I have always wanted to hear it, Lara." Miles could barely find his own voice, and the passion in his words gave Lara goose bumps.

She shuddered and closed her eyes. For the moment, it was sheer contentment just to drift on an exquisite cloud of pure sensation.

How long the two of them swayed back and forth, hardly moving at all, Lara had no way of knowing. Nor did she particularly care. All that mattered was that for the first time in years, she felt gloriously alive and fully intended to savor this delicious feeling for however long it lasted. But all of a sudden it seemed that the music had stopped and the band had already disappeared offstage to take their well-deserved break. Miles and Lara both belatedly realized they were the only couple remaining on the dance floor.

He drew a heavy breath and pulled reluctantly away from the intimate embrace. "That was quite a dance," Miles said unsteadily. "Why haven't we ever done this before?"

"You never asked me before." Lara looked up at him through her lashes.

"Maybe I just assumed you would say no," he responded with a faint shadow on his face.

"You shouldn't make those kind of assumptions, Miles."

"I shouldn't?"

"No, you shouldn't." Lara deliberately ran her tongue across her lower lip, wondering in her mind what might have happened if Miles had asked her to dance all those years ago. Would she have felt the same way she did at this very moment? Or might she have been blinded by other distractions?

"Are you saying that I would have been wrong not to ask before this time?" Miles seemed genuinely taken aback. "You actually would have said yes?"

She nodded wordlessly, just wishing that the music would start up again so that Miles could gather her back in his arms.

Miles stared at her in silence for one long moment, and shook his head. "Let's go outside for some fresh air." With a proprietary arm around Lara's slender waist, he guided her off the dance floor and out of the crowded room. Seconds later, the two of them were standing alone in the darkened gravel parking lot.

The summer moon hung far above them, bright and full against the night sky. Its reflection glinted in Miles's silver eyes as he gazed down at Lara. "I didn't mean to drag you out of there like that," he uttered roughly. "But the last thing we need right now is an audience."

Troubled, Lara glanced up at him. "Is something the matter, Miles?"

"You'd better believe that something's the matter," Miles groaned raggedly. "It's quite a problem, in fact. If I have to wait one more second to kiss you, Lara, I'll go right out of my mind!" He pulled her into his powerful embrace. "Come here, sweetheart," he said softly, and brought his hard mouth down to hers in a demanding, urgent kiss that brooked no refusals.

Chapter Seven

To say that Lara was unable to sleep that night would have been an understatement. Over and over, she mentally replayed the scene in the parking lot of Vinnie's Blue Grotto and was unable to find a moment's peace. And how could she? Lara shook her head and stared at the first rays of early morning sunlight as it began to stream in the bedroom window. Everything had changed since Miles's kiss. Lara shook her head. No, it was more than a kiss—it had been a devastating assault on her senses. Not even Jason, in all his persuasive attempts at lovemaking, had been able to coax such a response from her. A response that Miles had evoked so effortlessly just a few short hours ago.

Would the world continue to turn backward and topsy-turvy? Lara wondered incredulously. Was this the same mild-mannered Miles Crane whom she had blithely ignored throughout most of her childhood? Was this the same nondescript, somber intellectual who had faded so easily into insignificance whenever his younger brother entered the room? Lara was still reeling from the shock of Miles's raw sensuality. A sensuality that had spent years hiding unnoticed beneath a quiet, calm exterior. How was it possible that she could have been so blind? Jason, for all his undeniable charm and confident male swagger, simply did not possess that nameless magic ingredient. An ingredient Lara never believed existed until now.

They had stood there, in the parking lot, their bodies pressed urgently against each other. Miles's lips had burned a trail of liquid fire down Lara's neck toward the delicate skin at the base of her throat.

She had given an involuntary shudder at the sheer eroticism of the gesture, her fingers digging into the heavy cotton material of his sports jacket.

"Do you like it when I kiss you there, Lara?" Miles had rasped in a low voice she hardly recognized. "Tell me you like it."

"Oh, yes!" Lara confessed breathlessly. Her knees were actually shaking. It was sheer heaven to feel this man's hard lips touch her bare skin in such a blatantly sensual way. Miles's mouth traveled back up the sensitive column of her throat and possessed her soft lips once more. Unconsciously, Lara's lips parted to allow an even greater intimacy.

"Yes," he implored, a strange vulnerability coloring his deep voice. "Open your mouth for me, honey!"

Had men really called her "ice queen" and "frigid"? Lara marveled as she eagerly matched Miles response for response. Her arms tightened around his neck as he plundered the moist sweetness of her mouth with his tongue. Lara's body molded itself against his lean hardness and became shockingly aware of Miles's male arousal.

"Feel what you do to me!" Miles groaned and pulled away for a long, tortured moment. He stared down at her with an odd glimmer in his silver eyes. "You're driving me crazy, do you know that?"

For the first time in her life, Lara felt the exquisite power of her womanhood. "Am I?" she murmured in a silky tone, and reached out a hand to touch the hard line of his jaw.

Along that firm jawline, a muscle instantly tensed. "Was there ever a time you didn't?" came the taut words.

"I've already told you," she whispered faintly, "I've never been a mind reader." Lara's finger continued to trace a pattern across his lower lip.

The unconsciously erotic gesture was what finally sent Miles over the edge. "Come back here!" he uttered thickly, and crushed her mouth against his own once more with an almost desperate intensity. His firm hands moved down Lara's back to the base of her spine and pressed her hips against his in an even more

intimate embrace. Lara felt him actually tremble. She
was trembling too, as Miles's searing kiss went on and
on. She pushed away the lapels of the corduroy jacket,
needing to be even closer to him, somehow. She
needed to feel the warmth of his chest beneath the thin
cotton material of his shirt.

"Lara!" Miles exclaimed in astonishment, and
pulled back from her once more.

"What's the matter?"

Miles shook his head in frustration. "How can you
ask me such a question at a time like this?"

What on earth had happened all of a sudden? Lara
asked herself in confusion. A moment ago, Miles had
shuddered with passion in her arms, and now he was
staring down at her with a shocked expression on his
gaunt face. "What is it, Miles?" She paused in sudden embarrassment. "Have I done something
wrong?"

He rolled his eyes and gave a hard laugh. "Oh,
honey, I seriously doubt that you could ever do anything wrong."

Lara bit her lower lip. "Then what is it, Miles?" She
hesitated. "Why did you . . . stop?"

He smiled sadly and cupped her chin with gentle
fingers. "Where will you be two weeks from now,
Lara?"

There was a long, uncomfortable silence. "What
does that have to do with anything?" she protested.

"Oh, I'd say it has to do with just about everything." Miles's thin, weary smile did not reach his

eyes. "Another weekend, perhaps, and then you'll be back in Los Angeles."

Lara stared blindly down at the ground. "So?" What was he driving at, anyhow?

His lips were drawn in a tight line. "And by that time, you'll be living the kind of life that means so much to you." There was an awkward pause. "Who am I to say anything, Lara? It's a world that has made you so alive and happy, isn't it? You have a wonderful career there, and I'm sure, wonderful friends, probably even—" Miles hesitated for a moment, seeming to struggle for the words "—a special man in your life." The thought seemed to pain him, and this stunning possibility had an immediate effect on Lara.

"There's no man in my life, Miles," she confessed simply. "No one."

"I find that hard to believe." Miles's eyes narrowed with incredulity. "Very hard, indeed."

"Why?" Lara asked in thinly veiled annoyance. Did the man actually think she would lie? Is that how much faith Miles had in her after all these years? And far worse was the fact they were practically having an argument when the time could be far better spent kissing. Why did Miles have to talk about her returning to Los Angeles right now? Why did he have to remind her? Couldn't he just pull her back into his arms and let her forget about reality for a little while longer?

But Miles seemed intent on answering her last question. "Of course, there are other men in your life, Lara." Idly he kicked at a piece of gravel. "Whether here or back in Hollywood, there could never be a shortage of men chasing you. And why not? You've always been so bright and beautiful." He gave a resigned shrug. "Men just can't leave you alone."

Lara crossed her arms. "Oh, and I suppose you know this through some rare and magical crystal ball?"

"I don't need a crystal ball," came the taut reply. "Just a little common sense."

It was as if cold water had been splashed on her. "If that's the way you feel, then we have nothing further to discuss, do we?"

"No, I suppose not," Miles responded in a dull, metallic tone.

Lara bit her lips. "I'm tired and I'd like to go home now."

"Lara, wait—" Miles began imploringly, then stopped himself.

What did Lara see in his face for a fleeting second? Hesitation? Need? Some kind of secret inner struggle? But just as quickly, the moment was gone. "Did you want to say something to me?" she asked quietly.

"No." In that one stark word, a door seemed to have closed in Lara's face, and once again she was looking at the old Miles Crane. Stony and impassive. Somber and unreadable. He cleared his throat quickly. "You're quite right. It's late and we should really be getting home." He reached into his pocket and pulled out a set of car keys. "Tomorrow is going to be quite a full day." His tone was matter-of-fact. "I've got quite a bit of work at the office to catch up on."

"I'm *sure*."

Miles shot her a hard glance. "I would like to spend some time with Aunt Lizbeth, of course."

"Of course."

"It would be nice if we could both find the time." Miles walked briskly to the tan Mercedes and unlocked the passenger side, holding the door open for Lara.

"I have no trouble finding the time, Miles." She glanced at him sharply. "I have all the time in the world for Aunt Lizbeth."

But Miles didn't answer. He merely shut the door after her, and walked silently around to the driver's side of the car. Without another word, he started the engine and put the Mercedes into gear. The drive home was the most uncomfortable twenty minutes in Lara's life. The tension inside the automobile was thick enough to cut with a butter knife. Was this cold stranger the same man who had kissed her with such tenderness just half an hour before? What had suddenly happened? Why had everything seemed to go wrong at once? she wondered.

Miles didn't say anything. He kept his steely eyes on the darkened, shadowy road ahead, and there was that familiar tight line to his angular jaw. There was nothing Lara could think of to say to break the tension. This was a totally new situation for her. Oh, she had dealt with uncomfortable situations before. Hap

Harrigan was considered by insiders to be the most difficult man in Hollywood to work with, and yet, Lara had become adept at defusing tense moments on the set between the temperamental comedian and his beleaguered writing staff. Lara also had a gift for making people feel at ease at parties. Her friends all claimed she had a rare knack for keeping the conversational ball rolling, even during the most awkward situations. But here and now, in the car with Miles, Lara was completely out of her element. This was the first time in her life that Lara accepted the fact there was absolutely nothing she could say right now. Whatever was disturbing Miles lay dark and hidden in his own thoughts, and the man obviously had no intention of sharing those thoughts with anyone else.

Strangely enough, Miles acted as if nothing unusual had occurred the night before. Lizbeth continued to startle and amaze them with her rapid recovery. That afternoon, she was well enough for Nora to wheel her downstairs and out onto the stone patio overlooking the garden. There, Miles and Lara sat with her at the wrought-iron table, drank lemonade and ate delicate tea sandwiches.

"Oh, such a lovely day," Lizbeth exclaimed over and over with delight. "I feel twenty years younger."

Despite the tension that had existed between them last night, Lara was unable to prevent herself from smiling happily at Miles. No matter what might have passed between them then, this was another time and

Lizbeth was going to be all right. That was the important thing, wasn't it? Lara felt incredible relief that the woman who had always so lovingly filled the void in her life was growing stronger and stronger with each passing day. Miles seemed to have the same reaction. He nodded at Lara with the trace of a smile.

"You're still going to have to take things easy, Aunt," he urged gently.

"Oh, poo!" The elderly woman scoffed. "I refuse to be mollycoddled. And let's get on to more important matters." She paused. "Did you children have a nice time last night?"

The silence hung frozen in the air. Lara finally spoke first. "Yes, Auntie," she said, gazing straight at Miles. "I had a lovely time."

Miles's expression seemed to soften for the slightest instant. "So did I."

"Of course, you did!" Lizbeth chirped cheerfully. "Didn't I know that you would, darlings?" She looked at them both with sparkling blue eyes. "I'm sure the two of you must have equally delightful plans for this evening. Well, I hope you don't mind me being one very nosy relative."

There was a long silence. Then Miles said slowly, "The truth is, I have lots of work to catch up on this evening. I intend to be at the office most of the time."

"Oh, what a terrible shame, dear!" Lizbeth clicked her tongue sympathetically. "How disappointing for you both."

"Yes, it is." Miles continued to stare at Lara. "The entire situation is very . . . disappointing."

"If you feel that strongly about the situation," Lara said, staring back without wavering, "then why don't you do something to change it?"

A shadow passed across Miles's eyes. "Sometimes, there's nothing anyone can do," he responded softly. "It's what they call a no-win situation."

"What are the two of you prattling on about?" Lizbeth was mystified.

"Nothing at all, Aunt." Miles dragged his glance reluctantly from Lara. "Nothing at all," he echoed under his breath.

Miles left the house a short time later and did not return for dinner that evening. Lara was kept busy with Lizbeth until the old woman drifted off to sleep. Afterward, Lara occupied her troubled thoughts by watching television in the oak-paneled den. It was impossible to get Miles out of her mind, she realized cynically. Curled up on the old burgundy leather couch in her most comfortable sweatshirt and jeans, Lara was beginning to wonder if all the magical chemistry between herself and Miles had been merely a product of wishful thinking. Maybe that's what the man had been trying to tell her all this time. Sure. Lara's lips compressed in a thin line. The potent chemistry of too much wine, too much romantic music and too many years of being without a man's kisses. She stared blindly at the television set. Right now, some brainless detective program played before her eyes. It involved some lovesick secretary who had just murdered the sleazy crook who was blackmailing her handsome boss. Boring and predictable. Lara could barely stifle a yawn. Even in the unreal world of television mystery, women were eternally making fools of themselves over one man or another.

With a weary sigh, Lara clicked off the remote control and lay back on the sofa thoughtfully. For minutes or perhaps even hours, she started to conjure up the type of mystery plot she would write in a book of her own. She had always wanted to weave a rich tale of suspense, like her idols Agatha Christie or Daphne Du Maurier. One day, Lara decided firmly, she would leave the comfort and relative security of the television sitcom and write her novel. But at the moment, that time seemed like a long way off. With that thought stirring in her mind, Lara drifted off to sleep.

The next thing she knew, someone was gently covering her up with the multicolored afghan that usually folded at the base of the sofa. Lara's eyes opened drowsily, and there stood Miles, gingerly tucking the wool rug around her body. "Miles!" she murmured in a startled whisper, still not fully awake.

His gray eyes locked with hers. "I didn't mean to wake you, Lara."

"It's all right." She continued to stare at him questioningly. Since when had the man grown so solicitous? Hadn't he made a point of ignoring her all evening?

It was almost as if Miles could read her mind. He gave a heavy sigh and sat down on the couch alongside of her. "I owe you an explanation."

She shrugged. "Do you?" The words sounded more casual than Lara truly felt. Yes, he did owe her an explanation for his behavior. Darn right.

"Lara." He gazed down at her painfully. "Did you ever want something for such a long time that it seemed to be utterly impossible?"

"Yes." The word was dragged from her mouth. Involuntarily, the image of Jason was conjured in front of Lara's eyes. How she had wanted him almost all her life. How she had prayed, even after his betrayal, that her handsome fiancé would somehow see the light and return to sweep her away with him. It had taken years to stop wanting such a dream to come true.

Miles recognized the shadow that briefly flickered across Lara's hazel eyes, and a muscle in his jaw tensed. "I didn't mean to bring back unhappy memories."

"That's all right, Miles," she answered honestly. "The memories are still there, but they aren't unhappy anymore." That was true. Somewhere along the line, Lara had stopped caring about the past and about Jason.

"What are you saying, Lara?" His voice shook slightly. "What are you trying to tell me?"

She sat up slowly and looked at him intently. "Haven't you been listening at all these past few days, Miles?"

"Oh, I've been listening just fine." His expression was ironic.

In utter exasperation, she pushed the afghan aside and threw up her hands. "Take a wild guess, Miles Crane," she declared hotly. "How many men do you think I've kissed in the past six years?"

His faint smile did not reach his eyes. "I believe I'd need my pocket calculator to answer that one."

"Oh, you think that's funny?"

"No," came the abrupt reply. "I wasn't trying to be funny at all. You're beautiful and popular, so what else has changed in all these years?"

Lara's eyes narrowed. "Is that what you really think of me, Miles? Is the truth finally out, then? You consider me to be some mindless femme fatale, going through one man after another? That's what you think?"

Miles stared silently at her blind fury in total amazement. Then the harsh lines of his gaunt face began to soften. "You could have any man you want," he uttered slowly.

"Apparently not."

The total implication of her blunt response hit Miles with the impact of a sledgehammer. "Lara." He shook his head wonderingly. "Do you want me?"

She flushed bright red, overcome with an incredible shyness. Embarrassed, Lara averted her eyes. "Yes." She could barely manage a nod, her voice almost inaudible.

But Miles heard it. "Sweetheart." He reached out and tenderly cupped her chin in his hand. "Could I actually have been such an idiot?" Miles whispered in surprise, turning her face up toward his. "You really want me, and I've wasted this much time?" He brushed a strand of hair away from Lara's forehead, and gazed down at her. "Do you have any idea what it did to me last night to push you away like that?" Without waiting for an answer, Miles pulled her roughly against him and began kissing Lara with such raw, open hunger that it surprised even himself.

"Miles!" she breathed in sweet response, matching his urgency with her own need to feel his mouth again. She opened her lips to his like a thirsty flower, and his tongue plundered its warm sweetness with the new-found confidence of possession. She was completely and utterly his, Lara realized with heady intoxication as Miles suddenly pressed her back against the cushions. His hard, muscular strength touched Lara everywhere. Miles's hips molded against hers, his thighs pushing into Lara's with devastating evidence of the full extent of his male arousal.

"I've waited so long for this!" he groaned, beginning his own exploration of the sensitive cord of her throat with his strangely trembling mouth.

Lara wound her arms around his neck and allowed her tentative fingers the exquisite delight of running through the buoyant texture of his cropped pale hair. Meanwhile, Miles's lips were wreaking havoc on her already spinning senses, burning a hot trail of desire across her collarbone, and pulling aside the loose neckline of Lara's oversized sweatshirt to plant maddening kisses along the smooth satin of her shoulder.

Suddenly his caresses grew even more intimate. Miles's hard hands moved down along her sides and toward Lara's waist, reaching underneath the hem of the cotton pullover. His hands began to move upward along bare skin, and then stopped in shock as he realized that she was not wearing a bra. "Lara!" His voice was a rasp.

She looked up at him through lidded eyes. "Kiss me some more, Miles!" Lara implored.

"Do you think that's all I intend to do?" he uttered roughly, and pulled the sweatshirt away from her breasts.

"Oh!" Lara flushed with embarrassment, and immediately tried to cover herself with her arms.

"No, darling!" Miles gently pulled Lara's arms away to reveal the exquisite pink-tipped fullness she had tried in vain to conceal. "You're so unbelievably beautiful! Just let me look at you." Miles's eyes burned at the vision before him, and with a tantalizing brush of his hard fingers began an achingly slow caress of Lara's perfectly shaped breasts. While his hands cupped each creamy orb, Miles lowered his head against the heated velvet of Lara's skin, and locked his mouth over one pink nipple, teasing it to budding hardness.

Lara gave a convulsive shudder, and clung to him unreservedly, yielding to the heavenly assault of his unrelenting tongue. She was on fire for him, every pore was alive with the glow of anticipation. As Miles's powerful body surged against hers, she knew with shattering clarity that it was going to happen to her at long last. For the first time in her life, Lara was being carried away on a mad, dizzying tide of passion and nothing would stop the inevitable tonight. She knew it as Miles's breath grew ragged, and his tongue continued to expertly arouse new and shocking sensations from the core of her very being. This was why she had never given herself to a man before; until now, all other men had left her cold and unresponsive— even Jason. But now that the man who was her true match was guiding her so urgently toward the edge, she realized that it was impossible to deny herself the ultimate fulfillment. Unconsciously, Lara arched her body up to his. *I love you, Miles.* The words cried out from the shuttered confines of her newly awakened heart. *I love you, Miles,* she repeated to herself in a silent litany, stunned by the sheer power of her recent discovery. After years of believing she could never love again, Lara knew that whatever she might have felt for Jason was a shadow of the torrent of emotion raging inside her at this moment.

Somehow the sweatshirt had been discarded onto the carpet, and Miles's hard, tanned hands had moved down from her breasts, across the supple skin of her stomach. "You're like satin beneath my fingers!" he uttered thickly. "Sweet, smooth satin!" Lara gave a series of tiny moans with each taunting kiss his hungry mouth trailed across her stomach. "That's just the beginning of what I want to make you feel!" Miles's voice was so heavy with desire it seemed to catch in his throat. "It's just the beginning, darling!" And then, sure hands had expertly unfastened the button of her jeans, and in another moment, the stiff denim was being pulled down across the smooth columns of Lara's thighs. Seconds later, the discarded jeans joined her sweatshirt in a forgotten pile on the floor. Possessively his fingers traced a pattern along the frilly lace border of Lara's silk panties. "I'll make it wonderful for you," he promised. "The best you've ever known, sweetheart!"

Miles's own body shuddered with passion as he impatiently began to pull back the tiny scrap of lingerie. With renewed urgency, he eased his weight back on top of her, pressing his hips to her hips, his thighs to her thighs. The rough fabric of his slacks was the only barrier left between them. Somehow Miles had already shrugged off his button-down shirt, and tentatively Lara reached up to touch the pelt of golden hair above the waistband of his trousers. Miles exhaled sharply. "God, yes! Touch me, Lara. Please, touch me!"

Lara thrilled at the power of his reaction as her fingertips trailed along his chest and stomach. Daringly she allowed herself to lightly explore his body for the very first time and Miles could only tremble speechlessly above her. Never, Lara recalled, had she ever wanted to touch Jason in such an intimate way. In truth, she'd never had a true idea of what it meant to be a woman in every sense of the word until now. "I like to touch you, Miles!" Lara found herself whispering softly. Yes, of course she did, Lara told herself in secret delight. Who wouldn't take the most exquisite pleasure in touching the man she loved?

"Do you?" Miles's voice cracked, and he seemed so oddly vulnerable. "Do you really like touching me, darling?"

His endearment fell on Lara's ears like sweet rain. "I love—" she began, then caught herself barely in time "—touching you," she finished quickly. *I love you.* Lara had very nearly blurted out the confession.

But her erotic words were enough to make Miles lose what little remained of his self-control. With a low groan, he fumbled with his belt and then Lara heard the scrape of a zipper. Suddenly, his bareness was against hers. But instead of increasing her ardor, this new and alien contact made her stiffen involuntarily. The full implication of what was about to happen struck her with stark, blazing intensity. More than anything in the world, she wanted the lovemaking to continue, but now Lara found herself in the powerful grip of an unreasoning, paralyzing fear. A fear of the unknown. And at that instant, Miles's earlier words came back to haunt her. What had he said, just moments ago? That he would make it wonderful for her? *The most wonderful she had ever known.* Oh, Lord, is that what he actually believed? That there had been others? Others! Didn't Miles realize that he was the only man? The very *first*. "Miles, I—" Lara began to

stammer. Oh, God, this was so utterly humiliating.
But he must know the truth. It was important. *It
meant everything.*

"What's wrong?" Miles looked down at her in bewilderment, his body sensitive to the change in hers.

"There's something you have to know," she confessed haltingly. "Something I . . . have to tell you before we . . ." Lara gave an embarrassed pause.

Miles struggled to regain his control. "What is it?"
The words dragged from his lips. At once he was tense
and wary.

Lara tried to avert his burning gaze. "You were
going too fast, Miles." She swallowed. "It was all
happening too fast!"

Miles had always been a perceptive person, and instantly he was aware that something else was troubling Lara. Troubling her deeply. What was she going
to tell him? he wondered fearfully. Was it going to be
about Jason? He clenched his teeth. Lord, he prayed,
please don't let it be something about her feelings for
his brother. He would not be able to bear it. "What
else do you want to tell me, Lara?" His tone had
turned rusted and metallic. "What else?" He braced
himself to expect the worst.

"I've never done this before, Miles."

Miles stared at her blankly. "What?"

She lowered her eyes in mortification. "I've
never—" Oh, was he going to make her spell it out?

The impossible began to dawn on Miles. "You've
never done *what* before, Lara?"

"This."

And then the evidence began to tumble in around him. Lara's look of embarrassment, her stammering, and the sudden shyness. "Are you telling me," Miles said slowly, "that you've never..." Even he struggled with the words. "Not with anyone?"

"No one," Lara replied dully.

But that was impossible, Miles shouted to himself. "Not even Jason?" he demanded in harsh disbelief.

Lara shook her head. "Never."

"But you and he—" Miles's eyes narrowed into dark slits. "That's utterly absurd," he grated out. "The two of you were always kissing and..." Even now it pained him to think of it. *"Touching* each other."

Lara gave a pained sigh. How could she ever hope to explain this to anyone? "I...I told Jason I wanted to wait until the honeymoon." She could see Miles flinch at the words.

"And that's why you're still a virgin, Lara?" Miles clenched his teeth. "Because my wonderful baby brother left you at the altar?" Abruptly he jerked his body away from Lara's and reached for his trousers. "That's one hell of a quirk of fate." The bitterness in his voice was jarring.

"Miles." She touched his arm and Miles practically winced. "You don't understand."

"What's left to understand, Lara?" Miles stared at Lara's nude body with frustrated longing, and tore his hungry gaze away quickly. "That you carry a torch for Jason that won't let another man come near?"

"No, you're wrong." Lara shook her head. She had to finally say it. She had to make Miles know the real truth, as rending as such a confession might be. "It's something else. Something I couldn't tell anyone."

"What?" Miles asked tightly.

"The truth is—" she lowered her eyes "—Jason frightened me that way."

"God!" Miles stared at her. "Did *I* frighten you, Lara?"

"*That* was different."

He inhaled sharply. "How was it different?"

"I never wanted you to stop, Miles," Lara said with open vulnerability. "All I wanted was for you to go slower." She still couldn't face him. "It's still so new for me, you see. I never let...Jason go that far. I never let anyone else go that far."

A muscle in Miles's jaw tensed. "Why then, Lara? Why did you let me almost..." His voice died away.

"I'm not scared with you, Miles," she said simply.

"Why not?" There was a long pause. "Tell me, Lara!" he commanded urgently. "Why *not* me?"

No, she thought. She had exposed so much of herself to him already. Later, perhaps, there was time to tell Miles everything. When the risk was not so great. She loved the man, completely and utterly. But she was still not willing to chance revealing that, yet.

"I...I don't know why," she lied. "It just seems right with you, that's all." At least *that* part was the truth. It was absolutely right with Miles and utterly wrong with any other man. That was love, wasn't it?

"Oh, Lara!" Miles gathered her back into his arms with infinite tenderness. "I've been a blind idiot, an absolute fool." His fingers caressed her bare shoulders. "I was crazy to rush you like this." His hard mouth melted into a gentle smile. "We have all the time in the world, darling."

Chapter Eight

Not long afterward Miles had walked Lara upstairs and kissed her goodnight at her bedroom door. Several times he'd turned to walk away toward his own room, and then would give a reluctant sigh and stride back to Lara with a boyish grin on his face. "One more kiss, honey," Miles had murmured softly, and pulled her back into his arms for yet another passionate kiss.

It was almost as if the two of them were starting all over again from the beginning, Miles thought happily. That *was* what he had decided both of them should do. Back downstairs in the den, he had held her tenderly for what seemed hours, stroking her glossy hair with infinite gentleness.

"Why don't we just start all over from the beginning?" he asked with a glittering smile. Lara had given him a tremulous nod, unaware that despite his calm outward demeanor, Miles was actually shaking inside. The events of the past few hours had completely floored him. Never in his wildest dreams had Miles expected such a willing and uninhibited response from Lara. For years it was the mere stuff of fantasies. How many nights had he lain awake, dreaming of Lara MacEuan trembling with passion in his arms? Tonight, he had almost possessed her in the absolute sense of the word, Miles thought dizzyingly. When he had heard her unexpected confession, it was as if a dam had burst inside of him. Never before had she permitted a man to go as far as Miles had. And that in itself was a shattering realization for him. All the years gone by, when Miles had been wracked with a dark jealousy as he pictured Jason making love to Lara, had evaporated in an instant. Miles felt as if he was being given a precious gift.

He had taken Lara back upstairs, fighting every impulse to pull her inside his own bedroom and make love to her as he ached to do. But he had steeled himself with iron self-control. Very soon, Miles told himself, as he stood alone in his own room, he would make Lara his completely, as she had always meant to be. He had waited all these years, certainly he could stand to wait just a little while longer.

Miles tore off his shirt and threw it carelessly in the laundry hamper. One more week, he reminded him-

self gruffly. That was all the time he had before Lara
would fly back to Los Angeles. Back to the life she had
made for herself there. He grit his teeth. One week was
all he had left to convince Lara that her future lay
here, in Pine Harbor, and not the neon and tinsel
world of Hollywood. *One week!*

Things started out well enough on Monday. Lizbeth was actually able to join them for breakfast in the
dining room. It did not escape the woman's keen eyes
that something momentous had occurred between
Lara and Miles. How could anyone miss the way Lara
smiled almost shyly across the table, and blushed
bright pink any time Miles held her glance for longer
than seemed absolutely necessary.

"Miles, dear," Lizbeth murmured, "pass me
another slice of toast, won't you?"

"What, Aunt?" Miles was exchanging tender
glances with Lara.

Lizbeth chuckled to herself, and took another sip of
the weak tea, which was all that foolish young Dr.
Pedersen would permit her to drink. Did the two
young people sitting at her breakfast table actually
think it escaped her notice the way they were carrying
on? Miles was unable to carry on an articulate conversation without constantly breaking off in the middle of a sentence to stare into Lara's eyes. Lizbeth
could only imagine what must have taken place in between the time that Miles had stalked off moodily to
his office yesterday afternoon and right now. What-

ever it was, Lizbeth was delighted. Everything was turning out according to plan. "Oh, nothing, Miles," she responded to her nephew's vague question. "I just happened to notice a Bengal tiger on the front lawn."

"That's nice," Miles said, nodding, thinking how delicious Lara looked in that snug little powder blue T-shirt. Wildly he tried to imagine what sexy lingerie she was wearing underneath. Inwardly he groaned. How on earth was he ever going to make it through a long day at the office?

"Lara, dear?" Lizbeth casually spread more marmalade on her triangle of toast.

"Uh, yes, Auntie?" Lara was thinking how devastatingly handsome Miles looked in a three-piece gray summer-weight wool suit that matched his eyes. Back in Los Angeles, she was personally acquainted with numerous film and television actors, none of whom could hold a candle to the man sitting across the table from her now. Lara felt a tingle of anticipation, wondering what would happen between the two of them later on that night. Miles had promised that they'd spend the entire evening together.

"I was just curious, dear," Lizbeth began with a secret smile on her face. "Did you know that a rocketship filled with pink Martians just landed in the living room?"

"That's great," Lara replied, still lost in a dreamy haze.

Well, this is exactly how it should be, Lizbeth thought with pleasure. In no time at all, there ought to be wedding bells and then, who knows? The patter of little feet?

After breakfast, Miles walked to the front door with Lara, then pulled her tightly against him in a farewell embrace. "Later, honey," he murmured against her earlobe.

"Have a nice day," she whispered along the corner of his firm mouth, and pressed herself even closer against the hard, male length of him. He smelled of spicy after-shave and the balsam shampoo he used on his hair.

"I'm never going to make it through the day!" he groaned softly. At this very moment, the pressure of Lara's sweet young body against his own was arousing Miles to distraction.

"Good." Lara smiled mischievously, and planted light, butterfly kisses along the tense line of his jaw.

"You'd better stop that, if you know what's good for you!" he warned her shakily.

It was so delicious to have the confidence of possession, Lara thought with a warm glow in her heart. She watched Miles finally make his way to the Mercedes and drive off toward downtown Pine Harbor. If anyone were to ask her to name the happiest day of her life, Lara would freely admit that it was this day, of all days. Nothing could compare with the cloud of joy and anticipation on which she now floated.

Lara spent the rest of the morning in quiet conversation with Lizbeth. At one point, Dr. Pedersen arrived for an examination of his elderly patient. "Remarkable, remarkable!" he declared with a shake of his head. "I couldn't be more pleased. In another week, as amazed as I am to admit it, you'll be almost as good as new!" he marveled.

"I could have told you that." Lizbeth shrugged and winked at Lara.

But one thing the doctor would not waver upon was that Lizbeth still get plenty of bed rest. It was not a difficult prescription to fill, for the old woman soon drifted off to sleep, dreaming of wedding days and little children in sailor outfits.

It was left to Lara to walk the young physician downstairs. In the hallway, Dr. Pedersen smiled broadly at her and said, "You know, I've always wanted to meet you."

"Really?" Lara inquired conversationally.

He adjusted the sleeves of his blue jogging suit. "Oh, sure. Ever since Miles first mentioned you to me."

Her heart gave a leap. "Miles mentioned me?" How long ago could that have been? she wondered.

He perched a pair of aviator glasses on his nose. "It's a funny story, actually. Four years ago, we were playing a game of raquetball, and I accidentally clobbered Miles on the head with my racquet." He paused. "It really wasn't my fault. As it happens I am an excellent raquetball player. I once made all-county champion. Anyhow, Miles was knocked unconscious, and as I leaned over to revive him, the first words out of his mouth were 'kiss me, Lara!'"

Lara gave a start. "He said *what*?"

"Yeah, of course, the man had suffered a mild concussion and just as he started to regain consciousness those were the exact words he said. 'Kiss me, Lara!'" Dr. Pedersen gave a hearty chuckle. "I told the man in no uncertain words that even if my name *were* Lara, I had absolutely no intention of fulfilling his request." He grinned broadly. "But I've always wondered since then, just exactly who 'Lara' was. Now that I've finally met you, I can fully understand why Miles said those words."

"Uh, how interesting." Lara could barely manage an articulate response. After she escorted the cheerful young man to the front door, Lara could no longer restrain the singing in her heart. Miles had always thought about her! She was his first conscious thought after an accident! What an exhilarating sensation to know she affected a man in such a way. What a delightfully unexpected revelation.

Perhaps, had Lara never received a telephone call later that day from Mona Jackson, nothing would have gone wrong. Somehow, in the past six years, she had forgotten what a lightning rod for trouble Mona had always been. If there was an accident at an amusement park roller coaster, somehow Mona happened to be there. If the captain of the football team and the girlfriend of the captain of the swim team were necking in a car behind the all-night donut shop, Mona had seen it all. When an armed robber had unsuccessfully attempted to hold up the Pine Harbor Savings Bank, it was Mona who had stood directly behind the criminal in the express deposit line. In fact, she was known as Mona The Witness Jackson.

It had started innocently enough. The two of them were enjoying chef salads at The Sea Tavern, a favorite local lunch spot overlooking the yacht basin on one side, and the main business street on the other.

"You're just so lucky," Mona was gushing between mouthfuls of salad. "Being out in Hollywood with all those gorgeous movie stars. I bet you know some, right?"

Lara gave a faint smile. "Sure, everybody does. It's no big deal, honestly."

Mona rolled her china-blue eyes. "Of course, it's a big deal! What I would give to meet just one authentic superstar hunk." She shrugged. "I never left this town, Lara. The most exciting thing I ever did was to marry the captain of the swim team, and he's gained fifty pounds and lost most of his hair in the six years since graduation!"

Lara bit her lip. "Well, you know—"

"Hey," Mona interrupted her, "isn't that Miles Crane walking down the street?" She gestured toward the far window.

Lara turned around with a secret smile on her face, and the smile instantly faded. It was, indeed, Miles. But walking alongside him was the beautiful, elegant

Caroline Sinclair. "Yes, that's him," Lara said blandly. Well, in the first place, she quickly chastised herself, one should not jump to conclusions. They worked in the same office, didn't they? And hadn't she overheard them making plans for a business lunch last Saturday? Really, she quieted the hammering of her heart, there was nothing at all to worry about.

"Oh, yes," Mona was chattering on, "I understand that the two of them are quite an item."

"*Excuse* me?" There was an edge of steel to Lara's voice.

"Sure!" The other young woman waved her hand, totally oblivious to Lara's discomfort. "I think Miles took her to the Bahamas with him last Easter."

"*What?*" Lara watched the two retreating figures through the huge bay window. To her total shock and amazement, Miles suddenly stopped and looked down at Caroline. Lara had no idea what the man said, but Caroline wrapped her arms around Miles's neck and kissed him. The sight was enough to make Lara shut her eyes with total revulsion. It was more than she could bear. It was worse than any betrayal of Jason's. Far worse. Lara shuddered, completely sick to her stomach. Mercifully, when she opened her eyes again, Miles and Caroline had disappeared down the street. She couldn't stop shaking. All Lara wanted to do was disappear six feet under the floor of The Sea Tavern.

"Hey, is anything the matter, Lara?" Mona asked innocently.

"No, not at all!" Lara forced an artificial smile. "Why do you ask?" It was a nightmare, she thought dully, that's what it had to be. Could this be the same man who had trembled with passion in her arms just last night and wanted to make love to her this very evening? How could Miles do this? Sweet, honest, upstanding and moral Miles Crane. If Lara hadn't seen the kiss with her own eyes, she never would have believed it.

"You're as white as a sheet," Mona declared. "Are you sure nothing's wrong?"

"Quite sure," she replied through her teeth. Lord, all she wanted to do was to get out of here and crawl into a ball somewhere. Shortly afterward she managed to make some feeble excuse to Mona, and made her way blindly back to the house.

Fortunately when Lara arrived home, Lizbeth was still asleep and Miles hadn't shown his traitorous face yet. Lara locked herself in the bedroom for the next few hours and proceeded to cry her eyes out. How could this happen? She asked the tortured question over and over again. Worst of all, she trembled, how could it have happened twice—with two brothers—to one person? But hadn't this been her very reaction when Jason had so unexpectedly run out on their wedding day six years ago? No. If Lara was honest with herself, Jason's betrayal hadn't been completely unexpected. Had she chosen to watch for them, Lara might have seen signs of the young man's discontent and uneasiness. Jason had always been restless and enigmatic about the future. Lara simply had been young, infatuated and chose to ignore the subtle signals her fiancé sent out constantly.

But Miles had been different. Lara had finally opened herself up to love after six years of healing her raw wounds. Because Lara had reacted to Miles on a deeper, more mature level, the pain was far greater than anything she experienced with Jason. Particularly after his words of last night and this morning, Lara found this betrayal far more devastating. Miles Crane had been the only man to make her feel so vulnerable, so very aware of her womanhood.

Lara shook her head violently, and flung herself face down on the bed. If it weren't for dear Aunt Lizbeth, she would have been on the first plane back to California. But Lara was trapped. She couldn't desert her godmother. She had to ignore the raging torment of her own inner anguish. How on earth could she ever bear to look at Miles Crane again? And how in the world would she ever survive the next few days?

Somehow, Lara managed to drift off into painless sleep in the later hours of the afternoon. She was awakened in the early evening by a knock on her bedroom door. "Who is it?" she murmured drowsily.

"It's me, honey," came the laughing, happy voice on the other side of the door.

It was as if cold water had been splashed on her. Lara bolted upright in bed. "What do *you* want?" she asked in a rusted voice.

There was a pause. "What do you mean, 'what do I want,' Lara?" There was another long silence and then Miles said, "What's the matter?"

"Nothing, just go away!" Lara shouted angrily.

"Lara." Miles sounded unsure. "Is this some kind of joke?"

"It's no joke, you two-timing jerk! Go away!"

"Two-timing what?" Miles was incredulous. "What the hell are you talking about?"

Lara threw pillow after down pillow against the door. "As if you didn't know, you four-eyed weasel!"

"*What* did you call me?"

"You heard it loud and clear, buddy. Now scram!" She tried to make her voice stop shaking, but nothing worked.

"Open the door this minute, Lara!" Miles commanded.

"Forget it." She paused significantly. "Why don't you try the door to Caroline Sinclair's bedroom. I'm sure *that* one isn't locked!"

"Caroline? For goodness' sake, Lara! What on earth is going on?"

Lara stood up and walked closer to the door. "You must have had a real nice laugh today with Caroline. Did you tell her everything, Miles?" Lara's mouth trembled. "Did the two of you think it was all just so funny?"

"Lara." Miles's tone was dark and dangerous. "I haven't the faintest idea what you're talking about, but I suggest you open this door right now, and we can discuss it like two adults."

"There's nothing to discuss, Mr. Crane. I saw it all today, down on Main Street. I saw you kissing her."

"You saw what?" Miles boomed. "Lara, open up this door! I can explain everything." There was another long silence. His voice became more pleading. "Sweetheart, please! If you just let me in I can clear up this whole terrible misunderstanding."

"Don't make this any harder than it already is." Lara sighed painfully. "There's no possible explanation for what I saw this afternoon except the oldest explanation in the world."

"Oh, Lord!" Miles uttered raggedly. "Please don't shut me out like this, Lara! Give me half a chance to clear this all up. I know what you think you saw, but—"

"What I *think* I saw? Hmm, that's rich!"

"I'm begging you." There was an odd vulnerability to his voice. "I can explain everything, I swear."

Miles's own pain seemed so real that Lara would have been a callous creature to have ignored this final plea. Pressing her lips together tightly, she unlocked the door and stood back.

Miles pushed open the door and just stared at her for a moment, his baffled gray eyes taking in Lara's tear-stained face and rumpled blue T-shirt and jeans. With a gentle finger, he reached out to touch her cheek and Lara winced.

"Am I the cause of this?" he asked in disbelief. "Could I truly have caused you such pain, Lara?"

She crossed her arms resolutely, even now feeling drawn to Miles and wanting to believe whatever feeble explanation the man had to offer. "You were going to explain," she stated in a hollow tone.

"What you saw today," Miles said with a shake of his head, "was Caroline kissing *me*, not the other way around."

"Oh, is there a difference?"

"You're damn right, there's a difference!" Miles barked. "Is that what you think of me, Lara? That I'd make love to one woman and then go straight to someone else?"

"Yes." Lara turned away from him stubbornly, fighting all her instincts about the man's innocence. Fighting her common sense. "You—you suburban playboy!"

Miles quirked an eyebrow. "Me? Me, a playboy?" His lips actually twitched. "I've been called a lot of names in my time, honey, but never a playboy! Anytime but now, I'd be rather flattered." He touched her arm gently. "From clumsy bookworm to playboy. Now, that's quite a promotion!"

"I'm glad you think it's such a joke."

Miles whirled Lara around to face him. "Why do you think Caroline hugged me? Why do you think I even let her kiss me, Lara?"

"I already told you last night, Miles. I'm not a mind reader." Lara's traitorous body was already beginning to betray her, as Miles ran his firm fingers down over her bare arms.

"Obviously not." Miles drew a breath. "If you were, then you might have realized that Caroline was congratulating me, albeit somewhat overenthusiastically."

"What for?" Lara was instantly curious.

"Odd that you should ask," Miles said evenly, reaching into his pocket. "I told Caroline that I hope to be getting engaged." Miles drew a small velvet jeweler's box from the pocket. "It all depends upon what the lady says tonight when I propose to her."

Lara's jaw practically dropped to the floor. The complete rush of joy and restored faith was clearly evident in the pink flush flooding her cheeks. "Propose?" she whispered in utter amazement. "You're going to ask me—"

"I'm asking you now, darling." Miles gazed down at her with glittering eyes. "I love you, Lara. I've been in love with you since you were sixteen years old." He paused to turn her startled face up toward his. "Will you marry me?"

Chapter Nine

Lara's knees almost buckled. She looked up at Miles as if she was badly in need of some fresh air. "You want me to *marry* you?"

"I've always wanted you to marry me," Miles confessed. "Ever since I lost the chance to kiss you under the mistletoe that Christmas Eve."

"You *love* me?" The delicious reality of Miles's words had struck home at last. "You love me?" Lara's hazel eyes shone as brightly as stars.

"I feel I've been given a second chance to win you, Lara," Miles mused with a glint in his silver eyes. "Are you going to give me that chance?" He paused hopefully.

At that precise moment Lara realized that Miles was shooting in the dark. The man actually had no definite evidence of the extent of her feelings for him. He was a gambler, staking his fortune on the turn of a card. She admired Miles's courage.

Her smile was warm and genuine, and to Miles, it held the radiance of a thousand suns.

"Yes, Miles," she whispered softly. "I'd like to give you that chance."

His jaw practically dropped. "Does that mean you'll consider my proposal?"

Consider? Lara thought. What was there to consider? She loved this man and would marry him in an instant. This was hardly the time to play hard to get! Filled with bubbling confidence, Lara reached out and ran a proprietary finger down the front lapel of his suit jacket. "Sure, Miles," she murmured. "Give me some time to consider it."

He quirked a questioning eyebrow at her. "How much time do you think you might need?" He was wondering what could possibly happen after Lara returned to California. She could meet someone else, he thought wildly. Weeks, months could go by, and he still might be left hanging. Not knowing where he stood was driving Miles crazy. "Well," he said, attempting to sound calm and collected. "How much time?"

Miles was hardly aware that his tense fingers were biting into Lara's upper arm. When he saw her wince, he apologetically let go and waited for her reply.

Lara sighed. "I've considered it, Miles. The answer is *yes*."

For a moment, Miles was unsure as to whether or not he should believe her. "Did I understand you correctly, Lara? Have you just said you'll marry me?" His voice was not his own.

When on earth would the two of them learn to communicate more effectively with each other, Lara marveled. "What made you think I'd need any time at all?" She flattened her palm against the fine linen of his shirt, and felt Miles's involuntary tremor. "Don't you know that I would marry you in a minute, Miles Crane?" She toyed with one of the shirt buttons.

Miles's hand closed over Lara's. "You would?" He shook his head in disbelief. When she nodded wordlessly, he was still too overcome with emotion to speak. He opened up the small velvet box and drew out an exquisite marquise-shaped diamond ring.

"Oh, Miles!" Lara couldn't stifle a gasp. "How beautiful!" Was this all some wonderful dream or was it actually happening to her? After all the pain and emptiness of the past few years, was it truly possible for her heart to know such a moment of total contentment?

And then he was sliding the ring carefully onto her finger. "I hoped you would like it, Lara." He paused. "Of course I'm aware that these days a bride and groom should choose the ring together. My excuse is that I just couldn't wait. I saw the ring at the jewelers and had to buy it for you."

Lara wasn't really listening to Miles's eager explanation after she heard the words "bride and groom." It caused the most divine tingle all the way down her spine. She was going to marry Miles Crane. This tall, exciting, sensitive man would be her husband. They would share the deepest intimacy two people could know together. Lara felt herself blush again. How could she have ever doubted this man's feelings for her? How could she have carried on in such a way? She was utterly embarrassed by her behavior of a few moments ago. "I'm sorry about the way I carried on before," she began her awkward apology.

"Lara." Miles placed a firm finger over her lips. "I never knew until that moment just how much a woman could care about me." His eyes crinkled at the corners. "I'm very flattered that you think I'm... appealing enough to be a ladies' man." He hesitated. "Just as long as you realize that there's only *one* lady I'm interested in." Miles pulled her closely against him. "Now, let's talk business, honey."

Lara raised an eyebrow. "Business?"

"Sure." He gave a broad smile. "Business. You see, I made a proposition, which you accepted. It's time to make the deal official, and seal it with a kiss." Miles lowered his head and claimed her lips eagerly. But this was a different kind of kiss, unlike any Miles had ever given Lara before. There was an almost tender reverence to the sweet pressure of his hard lips. Lara parted her mouth to him as she had done the night before, but now there was a difference. Something new and wonderful had been added. Lara now knew that Miles was in love with her. His mouth explored hers with a passionate intensity that was beyond anything she had experienced before. With a groan, Miles's hands traveled down to her hips and molded her body against his. "I promised not to rush you, Lara," he muttered hoarsely. "But let me just feel your body underneath mine for just one moment!"

"Please, yes," Lara said with a quiver. She had been thinking much the same thing. She needed to be even closer to Miles right now.

"Lara, I've wanted you for so long!" He lifted her up in his arms and carried her over to the bed. With infinite gentleness, Miles lowered her onto the mattress. With a careless abandon, he tugged off the expensive summer-weight wool jacket and tossed it onto the carpet.

"You'll ruin your coat!" Lara protested.

"Who cares?" Miles muttered thickly. "All I want to do at this moment is kiss the breath out of you, sweetheart!"

He lowered himself carefully on top of her, pressing his lean hardness against her. She wound her arms around his neck and smiled up at him with shining eyes. Their mouths met and clung together like two people who had been without water in a dry and desolate desert.

With a low rustle, Miles raised his head several inches above Lara's. "I've never tasted anything like your mouth. It was made just for me, did you know that, darling?'' His voice was dark and low, whispering all sorts of tantalizing lovers' secrets.

"Oh, Miles!" Lara found herself whimpering softly, begging him for more. "Don't stop touching me."

"I won't," he breathed heavily. "There's so much more about each other we have yet to explore, Lara!" He slipped his expert hands beneath her hips so that Lara's body arched up into his. Once again she could feel his proud manhood surge against her softness, but now there was no longer anything embarrassing about it. It felt so good, so right. She swallowed convulsively and wrapped her arms even more tightly against Miles's neck. This movement unconsciously thrust her breasts against his warm chest.

"God, Lara!" Miles's body suddenly went tense, and he pulled away abruptly.

She stared up at him questioningly. "What is it, Miles? What's wrong?"

He reached out a hand to trace a path across her lips. They were pink and swollen from the raw passion of his kisses. She looked so bewildered and at the same time so beautiful that Miles's heart turned over in his chest. "Honey," he struggled for control of his spinning senses. "I can't let anything happen. Not until the time is right." He bent over and kissed the ring on her finger. "I'll make sure it's perfect for us, you'll see, Lara."

Now, Lara thought with a surge of excitement. She wanted Miles to take her at this very moment. She wanted to be his woman in the ultimate sense of the word. He had claimed her as his wife-to-be, and years of pent-up hunger could no longer be denied. Lara was confident in his love, and no barriers existed to prevent this sweet fulfillment. Why should they have to wait? Lara asked herself protestingly. She had already waited twenty-four long and lonely years. "It's perfect for us now, Miles," she found herself saying daringly against Miles's fevered earlobe.

"Lara!" he exclaimed in shock. "What are you trying to say?"

For a few maddening moments, she deliberately ignored his question, and concentrated instead on loosening his silk tie and unfastening the top several buttons of his shirt. "I just think you should make yourself more comfortable." She pressed her cheek against his chest. "I certainly intend to make *myself* more comfortable."

Miles drew her across his knees and cradled her in his arms with a deep groan. "Baby, you're ruining all my good intentions, do you know that?"

Lara shut her eyes for a long moment. "I can't help it, Miles. It's a kind of ache."

"It's an ache, all right," he agreed shakily. "But I don't intend to start anything we can't finish at the moment."

"Miles?" Her expression was so bemused and hurt that he kissed her quickly on the forehead.

"Sweetheart, please don't misunderstand." He smiled wickedly. "Later on tonight, I have every intention of making love to you until you cry out for mercy!''

His blatantly erotic words caused delicious shivers up and down Lara's spine. "Oh!"

He rested a possessive hand along her midriff, caressing the smooth skin underneath the blue cotton T-shirt. "Oh, *yes*, Lara!" he practically rasped. "But I want to take my time with you, darling—hours and hours." His hand brushed back and forth across her smooth stomach. "Do you understand what I'm saying?"

"Y-yes." Lara gave an involuntary shiver. Miles's overtly sensual promise thrilled her unbearably.

"I don't want anything or anyone to interrupt us," he declared with a catch in his throat. "But honey—" Miles hesitated. "As much as I want to lock this door behind us and make the world go away, there's something we can't forget right now."

"What?" The question was dragged from Lara's lips.

With an expression so lovingly tender that anyone who knew him would have been amazed, Miles gazed down at Lara, and brushed her lips softly with his mouth. "Aunt Lizbeth. Have you forgotten?"

"Oh, my gosh!" Lara sat upright and began to immediately tidy her shirt. "How could I have forgotten Aunt Lizbeth!"

Miles smiled vaguely. "I think it's safe to say that you might have had other things on your mind."

Lara glanced at the clock on the bureau. It was after six p.m. Where on earth had the time gone? "She'll be awake just about now, and probably wondering why we haven't come to see her!"

Miles straightened his tie, and flung his jacket over one shoulder. "I think she'll understand our reasons for being a little late." He drew Lara across the bed for one final embrace. "After we tell her, I intend to have you all to myself tonight."

"Oh, Miles." Lara's answer was nearly inaudible. "Yes, please."

When they broke the news of their engagement to Aunt Lizbeth, the woman's face lit up like a thousand Roman candles. "Oh, darlings," she exclaimed from her bed, "this is what I've prayed for!" There was a delighted pause. "Well, Lara," she demanded impatiently, "let me see the ring, dear!"

Beaming, Lara held out her hand, and the old woman clasped it in her palm. She examined the diamond critically. "Exquisite!" Lizbeth raised a curious eyebrow at Miles. "Three carats?"

"Four."

"Hmm, I'm very impressed!" Lizbeth winked at Lara. "Keep an eye on that ring, dear. I'm very tempted to borrow it sometime." She gave a girlish giggle.

Miles placed his arm around Lara, unaware of the serene picture the two of them made in the evening light of Lizbeth's bedroom. The woman stared silently for a moment at the two of them. What a hand-some couple they made, she thought. For years, Jason had always been her favorite of the two Crane men. His movie star looks and almost startling charm had endeared himself to his great-aunt from the very start. But Miles was different. He had never possessed his younger brother's looks or dynamic manner. Even as a child, Miles had been so quiet and unobtrusive. Liz-beth admitted with some degree of shame that he was not the kind of child whom she had ever wanted to hug. She had saved most of her affection for the far more lovable Lara and Jason. And yet, now, Lara was going to marry Miles. As the elderly woman looked at her nephew at this moment, she could see the change in him. He had never looked so appealing nor had Miles ever smiled such a contented, happy smile. He seemed suddenly ten feet tall and filled with a bright confidence. *The power of love,* she thought to her-self, wistfully remembering her own brief time of joy.

Quickly she cleared her throat. "Well, children, have you set a date, yet?"

Miles looked questioningly at Lara. "No, we haven't."

The sooner the better, Lara thought to herself, but glanced up at Miles. "I have a few loose ends to tie up in Los Angeles." Until this moment, her obligations to *The Hap Harrigan Show* had completely slipped her mind.

Miles took Lara's hands quietly into his. "I'm basically an old-fashioned guy, but I'd never ask you to give up your career for me. It just wouldn't be right." A look of hesitation appeared on his gaunt, angular face. "I'm sure we can work something out."

Lara's heart went out to him at that moment. She loved Miles enough to give up her career, and he loved her enough not to ask. She smiled to herself. Surely there were acceptable alternatives, other options. It wasn't as if she felt particularly fulfilled writing mindless fluff for a high-strung comedian every week. There was always her novel, and besides, if she wanted to continue in television, Lara had plenty of connections right here on the East Coast. "I'm sure we can." She nodded reassuringly at Miles, who gripped her hands even more tightly.

"When would you like to be married, Lara?" His words thrilled her ears. "Tomorrow? Tonight?"

Lara stared back at him, and realized that Miles was serious. "Isn't that kind of soon?"

Miles shook his head and gazed at her intently. "Not when you consider that I've already waited eight years, honey."

The raw, underlying need so evident in his deep voice made Lara tremble. "Sorry to keep you waiting so long," she tried to toss off lightly.

His gray eyes glittered. "Let's not wait too much longer, though. All right, Lara?" Miles's tone was dark and hungry, communicating a message as old as time itself.

"All right," she agreed just a bit too breathlessly and felt his hands tighten on hers.

"Well." Lizbeth studied her nephew for a long moment, and then regarded Lara's bright, flushed cheeks. "I'm suddenly a little tired. Why don't you children go downstairs and celebrate this wonderful news with a toast. As it happens, there's a bottle chilling in the refrigerator. It's been there since last Christmas, I believe."

"What a delightful idea." Miles kissed his great-aunt affectionately.

"An absolutely lovely idea." Lara was aglow with the utter joy of this day. She was home with the people who truly loved her, and Miles Crane was going to become her husband. At this precise moment, Lara doubted that she could ever feel happier. It was almost as if she had never known pain or betrayal from anyone. It was as if Jason and her engagement to him had never happened. With Miles, this was truly the first time.

Shortly afterward, Lara and Miles stood laughing in the spacious country kitchen. He had finally discovered the bottle of vintage French champagne hidden behind a rather unwieldy watermelon and several jars of olives far in the back of the refrigerator.

In shirtsleeves, Miles uncorked the bottle, which immediately gave a loud pop and started to spray over both of them. "Hold out the glasses," he said with an embarrassed laugh.

Giggling, Lara steadied her hands on the delicate stems of two fluted wineglasses, and Miles poured the bubbling, golden liquid to overflowing. "Here's yours." She handed one to him.

Miles hesitated, staring down into the glass. "I should say something very special at this moment." He gave a shake of his head. "But I can't think of anything clever or memorable. I can only say that you've made me very happy, Lara."

"Oh, Miles," was all she could reply with a slight catch in her throat, and held her glass out toward his.

"There's only one thing you haven't told me, honey," Miles began. But before he could finish the sentence, there was the sound of the front doorbell. An urgent ringing that almost shattered the romantic moment. "Oh, damn," he muttered under his breath, and set down his champagne glass on the marble countertop. "I'll get rid of whoever that is as soon as I can, sweetheart." He gave Lara a hard kiss on the lips, and strode with great annoyance from the kitchen through the dining room and out toward the entry hall. In the distance, Lara could still hear the insistent ringing of the doorbell, followed by the abrupt sound of Miles opening the front door.

While she waited impatiently for him to return, Lara set her own champagne glass down alongside Miles's and paused to gaze at the exquisite engagement ring. Only now did Lara appreciate the delicacy of the platinum setting. And how the diamond sparkled in the reflected light of the old-fashioned Tiffany ceiling fixture. Just then, she heard the sound of heavy footsteps returning toward the kitchen. "Miles," she began with a laugh, "you certainly got rid of them fast—" Lara was stopped mid-sentence by the stunned and shaken look on Miles's gaunt face. He seemed absolutely ashen.

"Lara," he uttered in an odd, rusted tone. "Look who's here."

"Hello, Lara," an eerily familiar voice said, and a tall, broad-shouldered figure suddenly stood in the doorway of the kitchen.

"Jason." The name was torn from her lips. She stared in disbelief at the man who had changed very little in the past six years. Still handsome, confident and smiling. The flaxen hair was longer, practically to his shoulders. There was now a beard and his clothing looked as if it had been worn for days.

"He's back," Miles added unnecessarily, and glanced at his younger brother with a tense smile.

"Yes, Lara." Jason's blue eyes sparkled. "I'm back." He paused. "Champagne? What are we celebrating?"

Lara continued to stare at him in utter disbelief. "Jason!" She repeated his name once more as the blood began rushing to her head and the room started to spin wildly around her. And then, Lara did something she had never done before in her entire life. She fainted.

Chapter Ten

The next time Lara opened her eyes, she was lying down on the leather couch in the den. A fog seemed to be clearing away from in front of her and Lara struggled to focus on the hovering form of the man holding a cool washcloth on her forehead. "Jason?"

"No," replied a hard voice. "It's Miles."

"I'm right here, Lara." Jason knelt down beside her on the Persian carpet.

"What happened?" she murmured dizzily.

"You fainted," Miles answered between tight lips.

"I fainted?" Vaguely, Lara remembered starting to fall and being caught in a pair of strong arms.

"I guess seeing me was quite a shock." Jason grasped Lara's fingers in a familiar, long forgotten gesture between them. "If it hadn't been for big brother here, you might have had a nasty fall."

"Was it you who caught me, Miles?"

"Yes." His mouth was set in a hard line as he watched Jason's hand gently caress Lara's. "Who else did you think it was?"

She quirked a puzzled eyebrow at the sudden harshness in Miles's tone. "Thank you for catching me and breaking my fall," she said softly.

Miles said nothing. He merely gave a brief nod of acknowledgment and removed the cold compress from Lara's forehead.

Jason still had not relinquished her hand. "Do you have any idea how fabulous you look?" He spoke in that same earnest, boyish voice that had mesmerized Lara as a teenager. "I mean, you've really grown up, Lara." There was a poignant note in his words. "You've changed."

"So have you," she confessed sincerely. Six years of endless summer had deepened his tan to a dark, rich bronze and there were tiny crinkles around his eyes and at the corners of his upturned mouth. He was as dazzling as ever, Lara thought, but it didn't seem to matter anymore. It was like admiring a beautiful statue. Nothing about Jason seemed real.

"I had no idea when I decided to come back home that you would be here, too," Jason was saying now. "This is just terrific." He grinned. "Like old times."

"Not exactly," murmured Miles under his breath.

"What did you say, Miles?" Jason asked distractedly.

"I merely said—" Miles stared at Lara "—things aren't quite the same as when you left six years ago."

"Oh, I realize I've got a bit of catching up to do," Jason confessed. "I still feel rotten about the way I just took off." There was an awkward pause. "Lara, there's a lot of water under the bridge, as that old cliché goes. What I did to you back then was pretty lousy."

"It was a long time ago," Lara said softly, removing her hand from Jason's and sitting up on the sofa. "Why don't we just forget about it." She was being completely sincere when she said those words. As far as Lara was concerned, the pain of Jason's old rejection had been long forgotten. She no longer bore her old fiancé any ill will.

"Do you really feel that way?" Jason marveled.

"Yes," she said with a nod, and glanced at Miles. Oddly, he didn't seem to acknowledge her.

"This is wonderful," Jason exclaimed brightly. "I'm going to like being home." There was a long silence. Baffled, Jason suddenly seemed to realize that the two others in the room had not said a word. The young man looked curiously at Miles, then at Lara, then back to Miles again. "So," he began conversationally, "I couldn't help but notice the champagne and glasses all set up in the kitchen. What are you guys celebrating?"

There was an awkward pause. Miles looked steadily at Lara, an odd expression on his face. "Would you like to tell Jason what we were celebrating, Lara?"

Was there almost a look of doubt in his gray eyes? Lara wondered in puzzlement. In just a few minutes, Miles had changed from a laughing, confident lover back into the enigmatic, guarded stranger of her early childhood.

"*Are* you going to tell him?" Miles added with an edge to his voice.

"Of course." Lara quirked an eyebrow at Miles. Why was he acting so strangely all of a sudden?

"Tell me what?" Jason interjected, digging his hands into the deep pockets of his faded, worn cotton windbreaker.

"Miles and I are engaged," Lara told him bluntly.

"*What?*"

"Lara and I are getting married." Miles stared at his younger brother with deceptive calm.

"You're kidding," Jason uttered slowly.

"No."

"Yeah, it's some crazy joke, right?" He looked as if someone had just punched him in the stomach. "It *is* a joke, isn't it?"

"No, it's not a joke," Miles repeated quietly.

Jason ignored him pointedly. "Lara," he entreated with an almost plaintive note in his voice, "you're kidding about this, aren't you?"

She reached out her hand and touched Miles's hand. It was cold. "No, Jason. I would never kid about something so important . . . so very important."

A vein in Miles's neck throbbed, but he remained silent and strangely unresponsive to Lara's touch.

Jason, meanwhile, shook his head in consternation. "When did the two of you reach this momentous decision?"

Lara gave a faint smile. "Not much more than an hour ago."

"An hour ago!" Jason exclaimed with a flash of his azure eyes. "An hour ago? Well, then, it's barely official."

"It's official enough," Miles finally spoke up. "Isn't it, Lara?"

"*Very* official," she agreed quickly.

"Hmm." Jason still seemed rather unconvinced. "I just can't quite picture the two of you as a couple."

"I don't recall asking you." Miles's voice was cold steel. Lara stared at him uncomfortably.

Miles watched Jason's eyes travel with renewed appreciation down along the slender, curved length of Lara's body. "Well, big brother," he declared, "maybe I haven't given you enough credit. You're just full of surprises, aren't you?" But it was clear that Jason was still mystified at the unexpected turn of events. "I suppose you want me to say that the best man won."

"Actually, little brother," Miles remarked coldly, "I don't want you to say anything. What goes on between myself and Lara is frankly none of your business."

Jason crossed his arms in amusement. "Don't lose your cool, Miles." There was another uncomfortable silence, and Jason gave a shrug. "So, is my old room still the same, or have you rented it out?"

"Don't be funny."

"I wasn't trying to be." Jason twisted his lips. "You know, big brother, in all the years I've been away, one thing still hasn't changed about you. You still haven't learned how to lighten up." He gave a yawn. "I'm really beat, and I haven't had a shower since Papua New Guinea. I'd better go upstairs and clean up."

"Don't let *us* stop you."

Jason rubbed his golden beard with an amused smile. "Touchy, aren't we, big brother?" He gave a light laugh. "Still trying to intimidate me with that stern, serious expression on your face, as if I was still ten years old!" He glanced conspiratorially at Lara. "Do you remember what we used to call him back then?"

Oh, Lord, Lara groaned inwardly. Why couldn't Jason just shut up right now? Did Miles have to be reminded of the way they both teased him all those years ago?

"Remember, Lara?" Jason prodded laughingly. "Serious Mr. Robot!"

"That was a long time ago." Lara looked embarrassedly at Miles. An eternity ago, in fact.

But to Miles, the world had already turned upside down. For all intents and purposes, the clock had just been set back eight years, and he was on the outside looking in once more. Never mind the pleading expression in Lara's eyes, he thought painfully. All he could think of was that Lara had seen his younger brother and had been so overcome with emotion that she had fainted dead away. Miles shook his head, as the cold reality of the situation jolted his heart. *Jason.* That had been the first name on her lips when she recovered consciousness. Not *his* name. It was *Jason* now, just as it had always been. All the tantalizing intimacies and sweet confessions of the past few days faded into insignificance now that Jason had returned home like a conquering Viking chieftain. The past six years had heightened his younger brother's appeal. Jason seemed even taller, stronger, more vital than ever. Miles's newfound confidence and romantic idealism were shattered as he watched Lara with Jason. No matter how much she tried to conceal it, she was still in love with him. How could he doubt it? And how could Miles possibly compete? He saw Jason smile his vibrant smile at Lara now and felt the bile rise in his mouth. Never had Miles known such a primitive, raging cold fury. He struggled for some semblance of self-control.

"So, anyway," Jason began, and winked at Lara, "after I clean up a little, why don't we all go say hi to Auntie?"

"Actually," Lara said nervously, "I think she's resting now. Maybe you ought to wait until tomorrow morning."

"Too much of a shock, huh?" Jason grinned. "Yeah, I guess you're right. Well." He shrugged off his stained, tattered khaki jacket, "That's okay. I've got a better idea, anyhow. Why don't I get a few six-packs of the world's finest beer to toast the happy couple?" He put a muscular arm around Lara. "Although, I've got to tell you, honey. I could certainly give Miles a run for his money!"

Lara could scarcely stifle a gasp. This was going too far, even for someone as careless as Jason. "That isn't funny," she began sharply, and then the words died in her throat when Lara saw the murderous look on Miles's face. The tension in the room had become so thick that she could have cut it with a knife. For one wild moment, Lara actually thought Miles intended to strike his younger brother. And she was right.

Before Jason could even react, a hard, angry fist crashed into his handsome jaw and sent him sprawling across the expensive Persian rug. He lay slightly dazed for a moment, then painfully propped himself up against the antique mahogany cocktail table and wiped his hand over his chin. "For God's sake, Miles!" he exclaimed when he noticed the blood trickling from the side of one lip. "What did you do that for?" He touched his swollen mouth and winced. "I never knew you had such a great right hook!"

Lara just gaped at the scene played out before her. Never, ever, had she known Miles to ever raise a hand in anger to anyone. And certainly not someone who was so much bigger and stronger. "Miles, I—" she implored.

"No, Lara," he gritted out between clenched teeth, "you don't have to say anything. Believe me, I get the whole picture." With a hard set to his jaw, he turned on his heels and strode toward the dining room, every muscle in his lanky frame taut with barely suppressed rage. He paused to look back at Lara for a painful instant. "I don't intend to stand in your way, Lara," he uttered raggedly between thin lips.

"What on earth are you talking about?" She took several tentative steps toward him.

Miles put out a hand to stop her. "It's all right. I already told you, Lara. I get the picture." He gestured at the half-prone figure of Jason. "He's the one you really want."

"*What?*"

"He's the one you've always wanted," Miles finished in a defeated, resigned voice. Before she could follow him, he had stalked away.

Lara could only stare after him in total bewilderment. "Miles, you don't understand—"

"What doesn't he understand?" Jason winced again as he touched his lower lip.

"Oh, shut up!" she stormed at him. "Why don't you mind your own business!"

"What did I say?" Jason inquired in a baffled, wounded voice. "Are you siding with Miles now? What is this, pick-on-Jason week or something?"

Lara glared at him in utter exasperation. At this instant, she wondered how on earth she ever could have been in love with this overgrown baby of a man. Lara almost could have laughed with sheer relief. Jason had done her the biggest favor of her life the day he had walked out on their wedding six years ago. She gave a sigh, and looked down at him. "Well, Jason," Lara began.

"Yes, Lara?" He struggled to his feet and gazed at her hopefully. "What did you want to say to me, honey?"

She shrugged her shoulders. "I just wanted to say, welcome home, Jason!" With a toss of her brown hair, Lara walked quickly from the room.

When she finally found Miles, he was sitting silently under a stately oak tree in the backyard. The expression on his face was dark and introspective. "Miles." She gently touched his shoulder, and to her amazement, he actually flinched.

"What do you want?" The words were dragged out from between his lips.

"What do you mean, what do I want?" In the dim light of evening, the flush on her cheeks went unseen. "How can you even ask such a question!"

There was a weariness in his eyes, and he looked suddenly older and more haggard. "I guess I can ask a question like that because as it happens, I already know the answer."

Lara didn't like where this conversation was going. Not one bit. "What answer?"

"Damn it, Lara!" he ejaculated hoarsely and turned away from the heat of her gaze. "Haven't I already made a complete idiot of myself? I'd never struck another human being in my entire life, and back in there I acted like some kind of crazed Neanderthal in a barroom brawl!" He paused sadly. "As if it would have made any difference at all what I did." Miles reached out to touch her hair tenderly. "How can I fight Jason, I mean really *fight* him? What the two of you have? What you've always had?"

Lara's hazel eyes grew as wide as saucers. "Miles, is that what this is all about?"

"I didn't believe it was necessary to state the obvious."

"Are you out of your mind, Miles Crane?"

He shook his head with pained resignation. "Not anymore, honey. I was out of my mind an hour ago. Back then I was crazy enough to believe that I could ever make you forget my brother. Crazy enough to think that the two of us could have a chance together."

"But you're wrong!" Lara exclaimed fiercely, falling down to her knees on the lawn to grasp his shoulders.

"Am I?" he responded dully, defeated. "Whose name was the first on your lips just a few moments ago, Lara? Who was the first person that came to mind when you recovered from your faint? I'll give you a hint." Now there was a bitter edge to his words. "It wasn't *Miles*."

"I was stunned, Miles!" Lara protested vehemently. "I was in shock!"

"Obviously." His jaw was set in a hard, implacable line. "The sight of my charming little brother was enough to send *my* fiancée into a dead faint!"

"That isn't fair."

"Lots of things aren't fair." Miles shrugged with feigned indifference. "Life isn't fair. I was a fool to forget that." He took her face gently between his hands and said, "You're so beautiful, Lara. I always wished I could have you."

"You *do* have me," Lara whispered urgently.

He didn't seem to hear her words. "I was so happy, honey. So happy that you just wanted me. I thought that could be enough, but it isn't anymore." He paused. "What I need from you, I'll never be able to have."

"What are you saying, Miles?"

"When I asked you to marry me, there was one thing you never said. I waited for those words, and they never came, Lara."

"What words?" As soon as she asked the question, Lara realized she already knew the answer.

"You never said you loved me." He shook his head. "I didn't understand why until I saw you with Jason a moment ago."

Lara groaned inwardly. How could she have been so incredibly dense? So unbelievably stupid? She chastised herself now. She'd been afraid to say the words to Miles because they had been magic words, too frightening to say aloud. Lara had been afraid it would somehow break the spell, and the fragile enchantment would vanish. But tonight, she would have finally told him. When they were alone, Lara had fully intended to let him know her deepest feelings at long last. Joyfully. In fact, she had been about to tell Miles just how much in love with him she was, when the doorbell had interrupted their champagne tête-à-tête. And Jason's sudden appearance had spoiled everything after that.

"Miles, are you really so blind?" she asked with a quiver in her voice. "Don't you already know how much I love you?"

"What?" The color drained from Miles's gaunt face.

"I love you, Miles," she whispered again, running her fingers across the strong line of his jaw.

"Don't play with me, Lara," Miles ground out heavily. "I couldn't bear it if you were teasing me."

"I'm not teasing," she said in a clear, honest voice. "Why do you think I let you touch me...so intimately?" Lara felt the hot flush rise to her cheeks in remembrance of their shared passion. "You're the only man I ever wanted to be so...close with, Miles."

He stilled her hand with his own, gripping it tightly. "Oh, God." Miles pulled her roughly into his arms. "You really love me, Lara?"

She trembled. "How could you have said what you did about Jason? How could you have thought there's a contest?"

"But, Lara," he protested hoarsely, even as his hands moved deliciously down to the base of her spine, "he's handsome. He looks like one of those rugged, macho film stars. Of course, there's a contest."

"Miles Crane," she exclaimed breathlessly, "I never wanted Jason to make love to me, but just this afternoon, I was practically begging you to take me! Doesn't that mean anything to you?"

"You really love me!" he marveled slowly.

"Of course I love you, darling!" Lara pressed her lips against the strong cord of his throat.

"Darling?" Miles practically rasped. "Do you realize that's the first endearment you've every said to me, Lara?"

Lara sighed against the sensitive skin of his earlobe, and felt him shudder. "For a writer, I suppose I haven't been very articulate when it comes to my feelings for you, Miles."

The alien glitter was back in his silver eyes as Miles studied her face. "I want to hear about your feelings, sweetheart. I want to listen to every sweet confession you can tell me." His voice was so vulnerable just then that Lara knew from that point on, there was nothing so deep and private that she could never tell this wonderful man. The first true love of her life. The only love of her life.

Daringly, she bit the already sensitized skin of his earlobe ever so gently, and this practically sent Miles over the edge.

"Oh, baby!" he growled and pushed her down onto the grass, his lean, hard length pressing on top of her. "Do you have any idea how badly I want you right now?" He lowered his mouth to hers, kissing apart her lips, and probing the moistness inside with a ravenous tongue.

Lara arched her body up to his, aware of every inch of Miles's stirring muscular strength.

"I want you." She gave an involuntary moan that excited Miles more than anything else could have.

"Right now?" he uttered roughly. "Right here in the dark, on the backyard lawn?"

"Anywhere," she admitted with a quiver. "How long do you intend to keep me waiting, darling?"

At the sound of her endearment and the blatant eroticism of Lara's words, Miles tore himself away with a hoarse cry, and sat up, abruptly. His powerful body was wracked with tremors. "God, Lara! You're driving me insane!"

She leaned against his shaking shoulder. "You don't have to feel that way, Miles. I *want* you to make love to me."

His breathing was rough and uneven. "Young lady, I fully intend to wait until we're married."

Lara looked at him in astonishment. "You *what*?"

He traced a delicate line across her lips. "We're going to have the most wonderful honeymoon in the world, sweetheart."

"I see." Lara quirked an eyebrow. "So, that's the way the wind really blows, is it, Miles Crane?"

"What's wrong, Lara?" He looked alarmed. "I thought you would be pleased."

"Pleased, hah!" Lara glanced at him through lowered lashes. "The truth of the matter is, you're the one who's playing with me, Miles."

He was flabbergasted. "I'm what?"

"Not five minutes ago, you accused me of being a tease." Lara carelessly tossed back her head. "Now, it develops that the real tease is you!"

"I'm a tease?" he boomed. "You think that I'm a tease, Lara?"

"Absolutely. Definitely. Without a doubt."

"Why?"

She gave a silky laugh. "You get a woman all hot and bothered and tell her all sorts of sexy, wonderful things and then, you suddenly pull back and say 'Nope! We're going to wait for the honeymoon.'" She rolled her eyes. "If that despicable sort of behavior isn't being a tease, then I cannot imagine what *is*."

"Lara," he groaned helplessly. "What are you saying? That we should make love now? Tonight?"

"Yes."

"Sweetheart—" He ran his finger down the line of her throat toward the shadowy cleft between her breasts. "As much as I love you, it really isn't the height of propriety to—"

"Propriety?" She compressed her lips thoughtfully. "Hmm, that's interesting. Here you can take little Miss Sinclair down for a hot time in the Bahamas, but—"

"What?" he practically shouted. "I did what?"

As much as the thought of Miles making love to his beautiful colleague pained her, Lara was willing to live with the knowledge of their affair because it had happened before their own romance had finally unfolded. Who was she to judge him for what he had done before coming into her life? "It's all right, I forgive you."

"You forgive me for what? Do you honestly believe I would sleep with Caroline?" He threw up his hands. "Lara, I did take Caroline down to the Bahamas last spring for a business conference."

"So I heard," Lara said dryly.

"I also took the rest of my law office, Lara." Miles shook his head in wonderment. "Did it ever occur to you, honey, that you weren't the only person in the world who carried a torch?" He gathered her back in his arms. "I've never been able to think of any woman except you all these years." He paused significantly. "Needless to say, it wreaked considerable havoc on my social life, to say the least."

"Oh!" A knowing smile slowly spread across Lara's face.

"As far as waiting until our wedding night—" Miles smiled back at her. "That really isn't such a long time to wait, is it? I mean, if I can hold out until tomorrow, I suppose you can, too."

"Tomorrow?" Lara stared at him in disbelief. "That's way too soon! I have plans to make, things to arrange—"

Miles placed a gentle finger across her lips. "Who's being the tease now, darling?" And he drew her back down onto the grass.

"Well," she replied shakily, "I suppose I could be persuaded to change my mind." She reached out her arms and wrapped them possessively around his neck. "Persuade me," Lara whispered.

Miles drew a deep breath. "I'll do my best, Lara," and lowered his mouth to hers at last.

* * * * *

Silhouette ❦ *Romance*®

COMING NEXT MONTH

#724 CIMARRON KNIGHT—Pepper Adams
A Diamond Jubilee Book!
Single mom Noelle Chandler thought she didn't need a knight in shining armor. Then sexy rancher Brody Sawyer rode into her life. This is Book #1 of the *Cimarron Stories*.

#725 FEARLESS FATHER—Terry Essig
Absent-minded Jay Gand fearlessly tackled a temporary job of parenting. After all, how hard could it be? Then he found out, and without neighbor Catherine Escabito he would never have survived!

#726 FAITH, HOPE AND LOVE—Geeta Kingsley
Luke Summers's ardent pursuit of romance-shy Rachel Carstairs was met by cool indifference. But Luke was determined to fill the lovely loner's heart with faith, hope . . . and his love.

#727 A SEASON FOR HOMECOMING—Laurie Paige
Book I of HOMEWARD BOUND DUO
Their ill-fated love had sent Lainie Alder away from Devlin Garrick—and her home—years ago. Now, Dev needed her back. Would her homecoming fulfill broken promises of the past?

#728 FAMILY MAN—Arlene James
Weston Caudell's love for his estranged nephew warmed wary Joy Morrow, but would the handsome businessman leave as quickly as he'd come—with her beloved charge . . . and her heart?

#729 THE SEDUCTION OF ANNA—Brittany Young
Dynamic country doctor Esteban Alvarado set his sights on Anna Bennett, but her well-ordered life required she resist him. Yet Anna hadn't counted on Esteban's slow, sweet seduction. . . .

AVAILABLE THIS MONTH:

 *Silhouette Romance* ®

DIAMOND JUBILEE CELEBRATION!

It's the Silhouette Books tenth anniversary, and what better way to celebrate than to toast *you*, our readers, for making it all possible. Each month in 1990 we'll present you with a DIAMOND JUBILEE Silhouette Romance written by an all-time favorite author! Saying thanks has never been so romantic...

The merry month of May will bring you SECOND TIME LUCKY by Victoria Glenn. And in June, the first volume of Pepper Adams's exciting trilogy Cimarron Stories will be available—CIMARRON KNIGHT. July sizzles with BORROWED BABY by Marie Ferrarella. Suzanne Carey, Lucy Gordon, Annette Broadrick and many more have special gifts of love waiting for you with their DIAMOND JUBILEE Romances.

If you missed any of the DIAMOND JUBILEE Silhouette Romances, order them by sending your name, address, zip or postal code, along with a check or money order for $2.25 for each book ordered, plus 75¢ for postage and handling, payable to Silhouette Reader Service to:

In the U.S.
901 Fuhrmann Blvd.
P.O. Box 1396
Buffalo, NY 14269-1396

In Canada
P.O. Box 609
Fort Erie. Ontario
L2A 5X3

Please specify book title(s) with your order.

January: ETHAN by Diana Palmer (#694)
February: THE AMBASSADOR'S DAUGHTER
by Brittany Young (#700)
March: NEVER ON SUNDAE by Rita Rainville (#706)
April: HARVEY'S MISSING by Peggy Webb (#712)

You'll flip . . . your pages won't!
Read paperbacks *hands-free* with

Book Mate • I

The perfect "mate" for all your romance paperbacks

Traveling • Vacationing • At Work • In Bed • Studying • Cooking • Eating

Perfect size for all standard paperbacks, this wonderful invention makes reading a pure pleasure! Ingenious design holds paperback books OPEN and FLAT so even wind can't ruffle pages — leaves your hands free to do other things. Reinforced, wipe-clean vinyl-covered holder flexes to let you turn pages without undoing the strap . . . supports paperbacks so well, they have the strength of hardcovers!

Pages turn WITHOUT opening the strap

SEE-THROUGH STRAP

Reinforced back stays flat

Built in bookmark

BOOK MARK

BACK COVER HOLDING STRIP

10 x 7¼ opened
Snaps closed for easy carrying, too

Available now. Send your name, address, and zip code, along with a check or money order for just $5.95 + .75¢ for postage & handling (for a total of $6.70) payable to Reader Service to:

Reader Service
Bookmate Offer
901 Fuhrmann Blvd.
P.O. Box 1396
Buffalo, N.Y. 14269-1396

Offer not available in Canada
*New York and Iowa residents add appropriate sales tax.

BM-G

Silhouette Romance®

A duo by Laurie Paige

There's no place like home—and Laurie Paige's delightful duo captures that heartwarming feeling in two special stories set in Arizona ranchland. Share the poignant homecomings of two lovely heroines—half sisters Lainie and Tess—as they travel on the road to romance with their rugged, handsome heroes.

A SEASON FOR HOMECOMING—Lainie and Dev's story...coming in June.

HOME FIRES BURNING BRIGHT—Tess and Carson's story...coming in July.

Come home to A SEASON FOR HOMECOMING and HOME FIRES BURNING BRIGHT...only from Silhouette Romance!